Let's Read About

Finding books they'll love to Read

Bernice E. Cullinan

SCHOLASTIC INC.
New York Toronto London Auckland Sydney

Copyright © 1993 by Bernice E. Cullinan.
All rights reserved. Published by Scholastic Inc.

Library of Congress Cataloging-in-Publication Data
Cullinan, Bernice E.
    Let's read about — : finding books they'll love to read / by
Bernice E. Cullinan.
        p.   cm.
    Includes bibliographical references.

    ISBN 0-590-47462-6

    1. Children's literature, English — Bibliography.   2. Children —
Books and reading.   I. Title.
Z1037.C9457   1993
[PN1009.A1]
011.62 — dc20   92-47362
                                                                             CIP

12 11 10 9 8 7 6   5 6 7 8/9

Printed in the U.S.A.   40

First Scholastic printing, August 1993

To my son, James Webb Ellinger,
who reads to find out
and who will argue with me about every point
but insist that his friends buy six copies.

Acknowledgements

First, I'd like to thank Kate Waters, at Scholastic, for her editorial guidance and shared enthusiasm for turning children into avid readers. Second, I want to thank Dr. Diane Person, first-rate librarian and graduate of New York University, for her discriminating taste and hard work on the booklists. Finally, thanks to my family, friends, neighbors, and students who allow me to tell their stories.

Table of Contents

Chapter 5: Find Books to Meet Your Child's Interests

Chapter 6: Moving Your Child Along

Chapter 7: Preschoolers

Chapter 8: Five and Six Year Olds

Chapter 9: Seven and Eight Year Olds

Chapter 10: Nine and Ten Year Olds

Chapter 11: Eleven and Twelve Year Olds

Appendix

Let's Read About

Finding books they'll love to Read

Bernice E. Cullinan

SCHOLASTIC INC.
New York Toronto London Auckland Sydney

A Choosy Reader

My son, James Webb, turned to reading primarily as a source of information. He went to books to get information and he took from them what he wanted to remember. He was, and still is, an active sports participant: always on the go — skiing, playing tennis, white water rafting, mountain climbing, or dashing about on roller blades or a snow board. As a child he did not read for pleasure nor did he read to relax. Instead he only read to find out, to know, to do.

I could get my son interested in a novel by reading aloud enough of the story to hook him; then he'd finish reading the book on his own to find out what happened.

As a young mother I needed to know what I know now — that there were plenty of books he would have liked if I had sprinkled them temptingly in his path.

An Avid Reader

Anna is an avid reader — a deep reader, an "aesthetic" reader, a reader who forgets the real world and carries on conversations in her head with people in the imaginary world of the book she reads. A scene in her home:

"Come to dinner, Anna."

"Yes, Mum."

"Come on. Do it now, Anna."

"Yes, Mum."

"I have your favorite chicken enchiladas."

"Yes, Mum."

"We're going over to the playground after dinner."

"Yes, Mum."

"Anna! I mean it! Get in here right now."

"Yes, Mum."

Anna's mother or father often have to go into Anna's room, literally take the book out of her hand, and lead her to the dinner table while she protests, "But I only had a little bit more to read to find out if Ramona is going to be sick at school. I was right in the middle of a good part."

Coping with an avid reader in the house is a situation many families never have the pleasure of facing. Anna shows the kind of deep immersion in reading that we want children to know — living in the spell of a good story.

Chapter 1:
Literacy in the
21st Century

At one time being literate meant being able to read and write. In the early days of our country, the only people in a community who could do that very well were often the minister and the schoolteacher. But times have changed, and so have definitions of literacy. Today literacy means reading, writing, speaking, computing, viewing, and being able to use a VCR, laptop computer, word processor, fax machine, answering machine, and other tools of communication. Simple descriptions of a literate person are impossible, but you can be pretty sure that your children are becoming literate if you see them doing some of the following things.

Signs of Literacy

It's a sign of literacy if you see your child:
- sitting half asleep at the breakfast table examining the side of a cereal box

- lying flat on the stomach with her head buried in the Sunday comics
- studying the win/lose column of baseball records
- devouring the fortieth Baby-sitters Club book
- poring over a book about tarantulas
- looking at the pictures in one of your news magazines
- playing games on the computer
- writing a note to a friend
- making a wish list of presents she wants

Readers come in all shapes and sizes; their tastes vary as much as human beings vary. Some children read fiction and will probably continue to read mostly fiction. Reading other types of material — such as the informational books my son reads — counts as reading, too. Kids read comic books. They read books from different points of view and ones with alternate reading paths, such as Choose Your Own Adventure. They read easy books. They read hard books. They read funny books. They read sad books. It all counts as reading and it doesn't much matter what they read as long as they catch the reading habit. As adults, we don't like to be *told* what to read. We want to choose. We may move from Stephen King to Anne Tyler to Amy Tan to Maya Angelou to Jane Smiley to Toni Morrison to Shakespeare to Proust. But we decide. Kids want the same courtesy. We are willing to consider books recommended by a person we trust; so are children.

What Do Readers Do?

- Readers choose what they read. They read about things that interest them.
- Readers bring their background knowledge about a topic with them when they read. The more they know, the better they read and the more they get out of reading.
- Readers bring their own background of experience to bear on what the words mean. They go back and forth between the words and their experience to create meaning.
- Readers read for meaning. They skip over words they don't know. Good readers don't need to read every word to understand what they read.
- Readers read with a dictionary. If there's a word they can't figure out from the words around it and it interferes with understanding, they look it up.
- Readers read when they're happy, sad, sleepy, tired, bored, curious, and angry. Reading fits every mood.
- Readers read to find out, to live in another world, to explore relationships, to see what life will be like in a few years, to learn about

things, to make them laugh and cry.

- Readers like to take part in their literature. They like to become the voice speaking inside a text. They feel as if they *are* the character and that what happens to the character is really happening to them.

What do the new definitions of reading and literacy mean for parents? First, it means that we recognize reading as a joyful experience — readers become deeply absorbed. Second, it means we don't quiz readers to see if they found the right answer. Third, it means that readers go to books for all sorts of reasons — none more valid than the next. Finally, it means we search for books that meet and expand their interests. If we do these things, we can breathe the essence of literature into readers' lives and make readers for life. The books do exist and this book should help you find them no matter what your child's age or interests.

How This Book Can Help

Use *Let's Read About . . .* to find a book for a child that is sure to get him excited about reading.

Use it to choose a book for a child's gift or to expand the number of good books you've already collected.

Use it to guide you at the library when you're looking for that special book to tempt a picky reader.

This book is for people who want to hook a so-so reader as well as for those who want to feed books to the omnivorous reader.

Children get excited about reading when they are just beginning to learn how to read. They lose their enthusiasm, however, if what we give them to read is what they call "bor-ing!" When a child strikes out on her own as a reader, it's even more important to see that she finds really good books during this critical period.

One way to hook a reader is to give him a book that grabs his attention, whether it's about bugs, bats, or bees. It may need to be a really funny book, or a biography of a cartoonist — if he's excited about comic books. He may say, as my son said, "I didn't know they had books on water scooters." Find books to help children explore their world.

My purpose for writing this book is that I want parents to know what it takes to raise a reader. I want you to know the joy that comes from doing so. I want you to know how to create the magic that permeates the child's world when he becomes absorbed in a terrific book. I want you and your child to share in the splendor of lives we could never lead. I want you to recognize the look in a child's eye when he believes that King

Arthur once lived and that the world is a better place because he was here.

This book answers the question, "What do I do now?" The booklists are a jumping-off point. The lists contain books that we know, they are tried and true — they've worked to turn many children into readers and they'll probably work for your child, too.

How do I make choices? There are so many demands for children's time, interest, and money that we parents hardly know which way to turn. Should we spend money on computer games, videocassettes, CD players, audiotapes, or books? Is it a good investment to spend eighteen dollars on a book? How do I decide which book is the right one? That's where *Let's Read About* . . . can help you. You will find something interesting for every child at every age level.

The booklists are organized by age group and within age by topic or theme. Of course, age group assignments are not ironclad. Children read "over their heads" about topics they love. Your child may read from lists both older and younger than he is. But the lists are a place to start.

Your child will lead you by the hand once he's caught the reading habit. We chose the booklist topics because they are the ones many children ask for in classrooms, libraries, and bookstores. Children often say, "I want a book about a person just like me." That's the time to pick up a book by Beverly Cleary, or Virginia Hamilton, or Lois Lowry.

When a child says, "I want to be an astronaut," you can find the book by Sally Ride. When they ask for another horse story, you can give them the new poetry book about horses, *The Music of Their Hooves* by Nancy Springer. Whatever the interests, you'll find books to meet them.

When children have learned to read and want to try out their wings as readers, that's when the real fun begins. That's when reading is contagious. Let's start an epidemic!

Chapter 2:
Make Your Home a
Comfortable Place to Read

In the midst of a chaotic, topsy-turvy world, you can create an island of tranquility, free of commotion. Your children deserve it and so do you. Books and reading help to slow the pace of life to a reasonable speed. Actually, books and reading serve two purposes at home: They become the reason for establishing a peaceful period and the means for doing it at the same time.

Create a Reading Environment

Read aloud to your child. It's never too early to begin; it's never too late to start. Children are never too old to be read to; they're never too young to be read to. Reading aloud is the single most important factor in developing a child's interest and ability in reading. No activity does more than reading aloud to prepare a child for success in school. Readers are learners.

Continue to read aloud after your child learns

to read alone. Children can always understand more complex material than they are able to read. Furthermore, they need to hear what good reading is supposed to sound like — and you are providing the model.

Tips For Reading Aloud

1. Read aloud every day. Better, several times a day.
2. Read aloud something you know and really like. Your enthusiasm is contagious.
3. Choose a story, poem, or news item to grab your child's interest.
4. Cut the session short if interest lags.
5. Link the story to life and other books.
6. Ask your child to predict the outcome.
7. Talk about the book.

"It is bedtime but you may keep your light on and read for half an hour." When you say this to your children they think you're giving them a gift of extra time to stay awake. What you are really giving them is a gift that will last a lifetime — the habit of reading yourself to sleep.

Talk about whatever your child is reading. Talk about what you are reading. If you see your child engrossed in the cereal box, talk about what it says. Cereal boxes, by the way, are the most commonly read pieces of print in the country. Read the cereal box together. Advertisers want to fill every inch of space on cartons; read what they have to say. You are turning your child into a compulsive reader — the kind of person who is compelled to read whatever print is in front of her.

Read aloud interesting bits of language whenever you find them. Call attention to the funny little tidbits you find in the newspaper, magazine, or other things you might be reading. Jim Trelease, author of *The New Read-Aloud Handbook*, says the expression, "Hey, listen to this!" caused him, his brothers, and his children to become readers.

Leave books around. Stack books beside the bed. Stack books by the bathtub. Put books in a basket beside the toilet. Keep books in the van or car. Carry books in your carry-all bag.

Leave magazines and newspapers lying around. Children pick up whatever is lying in front of them — *Time* magazine, *Newsweek*, or the daily newspaper — and flip through the pages. It helps if there are some children's magazines, too, but your own magazines are fine. Children skim the headlines, look at the photographs, glance at interesting items. We never get a prize for tidiness in housekeeping but we create our own prize when we raise a reader. A print-filled home looks lived in.

Put a sign on the refrigerator: We are going to

Reading on the Run

Five year old Katie and I rode in the backseat of the car on the way home from the city. We had a copy of *Is Your Mama a Llama?* by Deborah Guarino to make the ride more fun. I read the first few pages and invited Katie to join in with me on the repeated phrases.

"Is your mama a llama?" I asked my friend Fred.

"No she is not," is what Fred said. Katie and I pointed to each word as she said the phrases with me. Then I said, "Your turn."

Katie said/read the rest of the repeated phrases alone; I read the other parts. Certainly Katie memorized the words she was saying but she was acting like a reader. If she does this often enough, she'll pick up reading on her own.

the library. What books do you want? Mom: a good mystery or fashion book. Dad: a book about Mexico or Arkansas. Jeremy: a joke book. Alicia: a book about cats.

Put maps on the wall. All reading doesn't come from books. If Dad or Mom is on a trip, follow the itinerary on the wall map. If Grandma and Grandpa live in another city or state, mark the spot where they live. If a friend moves away, write the friend's name on a Post-It and stick it on the map.

Put up a bulletin board. Stick postcards on it. If you receive a postcard from Aunt Tia, pin it up on the corkboard and mark the spot on the wall map to show where it's from.

Read rap lyrics, song lyrics, verses, riddles, jokes, commercials, and poetry aloud. Use Jim Trelease's line, "Hey, listen to this!" and read to anyone in listening range.

Help create a private space for your child. Children feel cozy in their own little world when they're wrapped up in a blanket hiding behind the sofa. Help them create a snug-as-a-bug-in-a-rug nest — some place to take books. It might serve as a good "time-out" spot, too. Let your child spend time in her cozy spot by herself.

Children imitate the behaviors they see. You are your child's model — she will do the same things you do.

I'll Give You a Clue

Six-year-old Erminda was helping her five-year-old brother Eugene learn to read. The print said, "I can jump." Eugene read the word "I" but was stumped by the next word. Erminda said, "I'll give you a hint. He's married to Barbie."

Establish Time to Read

Set one half hour of reading time for the whole family — no TV. The sky will not fall. The world will not come to an end. Your children will not run away from home! This is the time when everybody reads. You read, too. Eventually you'll discover that the half hour is expanding.

Establish a regular time to read. Bedtime works well for many — but another good time is when it's not quite time for a meal. The kids are fussy and hungry, and you want to hold them off. Stories work wonders at this special time. If one child is learning to read independently, this is a good time to practice. Let him read to the others — or stop and let her fill in the missing word. It's a special time to give attention to a child.

Build Memories

Children are with us for a very short period in the span of a lifetime. What we do during their brief stay determines, to a large extent, what they do with the rest of their lives. Parents who provide memorable book experiences send their children into the world supplied with a trunk filled with loving memories. Children can pull memories from that trunk to savor and to enjoy those experiences time and again. The memories strengthen, support, and undergird the child through a lifetime.

Show your child that you value what he does. Many schools have writing programs that result in a "published" book with your child's name on it as the author. Make that book a family treasure: Display it in a place of honor. Put it with other books from the library and bookstore, call it a "real" book, and choose it for reading aloud.

A child who associates books with love is a happy child. When you read to a child from an early age, he develops a positive attitude toward reading. The warmth and security that a child feels goes with him as he learns to read on his own, as he becomes an independent reader and reads for information, as he reads to make a

The Gates Are Closing

Joe, father of Eileen, Kerry, and Brian, had a special way of announcing to his children that it was time for their bedtime story. He would sit on the couch and say, "The gates are closing . . . the gates . . . sss . . . are . . . cloooo . . . sing" as he made a big circle of his arms for the nightly reading session. The children rushed to get ready for bed and to get inside the circle of arms that snapped closed when all three were safely inside. Eileen ran like crazy to get inside the circle; it seemed like a matter of life and death to her. Eileen recalls with pleasure the memories of stories told and books read inside the closing gates.

living, as he reads for pleasure. It never leaves.

Books are the most memorable artifact of childhood. Children seem to latch onto certain books and carry them in their hearts for the rest of their lives. I ask my students at NYU to recall a memory from childhood that had something to do with learning to read or write. Instantly I can tell who had memorable book experiences — more from the way they look than from what they say. The ones who recall happy book experiences get a look on their face — like the Mona Lisa smile — somewhere between reverie and dreaming. They just drift off into a private world as if they're disappearing into some story read to them 20–30 years ago. Anything that powerful is worth passing on.

A Birthday Card Celebrates Memories

My daughter, Janie, sent this card to me on my birthday:

You did so many things for me when I was growing up. Maybe the ones I remember best seemed pretty ordinary to you — like reading to me every night in bed. I remember thinking that Curious George had more fun than I did even though he got in trouble. And Dr. Seuss taught me what loyalty was when Horton sat on those eggs to hatch them. Henry Reed and Nancy Drew seemed like kids down the street. You made me feel important and loved with everything you did. For all the times I forgot to tell you then, thanks Mom.

Janie

Chapter 3:
Discover Your
Child's Interests

Spend Time with Your Child

Listen to your child when she talks to you. Listen to your child when she talks to her friends. It's easy to be a silent driver when it's your turn for the car pool. Children soon forget that you are there and talk freely to their friends. It's a good time to pick up ideas about what your child is interested in.

Make a special date with your child.

Talk with your child about television programs. Find books that answer questions raised by TV. If your child asks you questions and you don't know the answer, say, "Let's go to the library and see what we can find out."

Find out what your child thinks about the TV shows she or he watches. If you watch the programs, too, you have a better basis for a conversation. Discussing what she sees on television helps your child clarify what the programs mean and how the values relate to your own lives.

Make Special Dates

Peter, my godchild's father, makes special dates with each of his three children. Once a month, each child has her/his father's undivided attention for an entire day. They go shopping, to sports events, movies, plays, museums, or whatever strikes their fancy. They have lunch together. Peter doesn't have to ask about the kind of books to buy for gifts.

Ask your child about what he is reading in school. If possible, read the book yourself. Talking about books brings unexpected results — close sharing between reading partners.

Ask what your child is studying in school. There are excellent books set in every historical period. There are excellent nonfiction books on every school topic. You will find some special books in the booklists to match to your child's school-related study.

Talk to your child's teacher. Teachers often have insights about a child's special interests.

Put up a sign-up sheet on the refrigerator. Make a column for each family member and leave room to write: Books I want. Things I want to learn about. Places I'd like to go.

It's pretty obvious: If you want to discover your child's interests, spend time with her.

Expand Your Child's Interests

Take a look at the world through the eyes of a child. Talk enthusiastically about things you observe: Do you see the rainbow in that soap bubble? Is the light shining through the windowpane like a prism? Are those things growing in the crack in the sidewalk really flowers or moss?

Child prodigies usually have someone to plant seeds of interest and to support their growth. Pianist Van Cliburn's mother listened to classical music on the radio and he soaked up the music along with the food he ate and the air he breathed. As a child, artist Jerry Pinkney liked to draw and his mother said, "Well if that's what Jerry wants that's what I want, too."

If your child sees the space shuttle blast off on TV, go to the library and get books on space shuttles, space travel, biographies of astronauts. Even Robert Heinlein's classic, *Have Space Suit, Will Travel*, would be fun to read because it was written before we knew much about outer space. Talk about new science fiction, such as H. M. Hoover's *Delikon*. Your child will like what you like.

Just Like Dad

Charley's dad devotes time to Charley because he thoroughly enjoys him. They track animals, spot wild geese, hunt, and camp out. Charley likes what his dad likes. His interests are not only recognized by his father, they are partially shaped by him. Because Charley enjoys the kinds of things he does with his father he reads outdoor adventure and survival books like *Hatchet* and *Tracker* (by Gary Paulsen).

Chapter 4:
Know Your Child's Level
of Understanding

If you know your child's level of intellectual development, you'll more likely pick out toys, books, and games at the right level. A book that bores a five year old may fascinate a seven year old. And it's unusual for an eleven year old to be interested in a wonderful picture book you've just discovered. Children don't go back and read things they consider to be "baby books" unless they are old favorites that bring back happy memories. Part of a child's intelligence is determined by the stimulation we provide. The ideal is to choose books that are interesting for plot and/or subject and that are increasingly challenging in vocabulary and structure.

We learn in many ways — from firsthand experience and from vicarious experiences. Books open windows. They show us the world we cannot experience firsthand. Books and experiences teach new vocabulary and concepts.

Children are avid language learners; they learn from their experience and from those around them.

A Big Sandbox

Four-year-old Jenny loved her sandbox. It was her favorite place to play. She would spend hours endlessly shoveling sand into pails and making sand castles. She filled buckets full of sand, made sand pies, and drove her trucks through sand roads. One day Grammy and Grandpa took her to a beach where the sand stretches a mile wide and several miles long. Jenny walked with her grandparents onto the beach, then she stopped and stared, absolutely amazed. She looked up at Grammy and Grandpa and said, "What a big, big sandbox."

The following sections draw upon what children are interested in at various ages and suggest what they are most apt to like in books. Age levels vary. Use these ideas as a guide but turn directly to your child for specific leads.

Preschoolers

• Want to see people like themselves in books. They like to point to mommies, daddies, ba-

Then I'll Do It Myself — Just Like You

Vivian was preparing dinner when her four-year-old son Chris asked, "Mommy can you read me a book?" When Vivian told him to wait, Chris volunteered to go get the book. Chris left but did not come back.

Vivian explains: It was very quiet and I wondered what he was doing. So I went to his room to check. There he is sitting on the floor with the dog next to him. He has a book on his lap and he's reading to the dog! He asks the dog questions and then he gives the answer. He shows the pictures to the dog and slides his finger under the words just like I do. I can't believe that he's going through the exact same motions I use when we read together.

bies, sister, brother. If the books represent different cultural groups you are acquainting them with the varied nature of their real world.

• Like simple folktales.

There is real reason for the repetition of three in the ancient folktales — three is easy to remember. Stories about the *three* bears, the *three* billy goats gruff, the *three* little pigs are just the right length and have the right ingredients for young listeners: simple plots, happy endings.

- Like toy books, action books, lift-the-flap books.

  Young children sit still for a limited time but if they can participate in turning the pages, lifting a flap, or patting a bunny, they pay attention longer. Reading to a child increases his attention span markedly.

- Relate books to real life.

  Children make a huge cognitive leap when they recognize that the flat pictures in books represent the three-dimensional apple, dog, or person in real life. Once they know that books reflect life, they make numerous connections. They play the parts of book characters in real life, they see things in books that are like their lives, and they re-create episodes from books in their real lives.

- Like animals that talk.

  Feed the fancy. Get talking animal books.

Five and Six Year Olds

- Believe that fairy tale characters once lived.

  Children this age think that the stories in books are "real" and that Cinderella lived "a long time ago." They like the idea of a prince and princess and accept the ending "they lived happily ever after" as true and satisfying.

- Are innately curious about their world.

  Five and six year olds want to know how their world works, how print works, what makes clocks tick. They explore books to find out about their world.

Tamara Loses a Tooth

Six-year-old Tamara lost a tooth on Martin Luther King Day. Her mother, Gail, was prepared for this momentous occasion with *Arthur Loses a Tooth* by Marc Brown and *One Morning in Maine* by Robert McCloskey plus a few other tooth fairy books. Tamara listened quietly to the stories but she wanted to talk about what she'd learned in school — that Martin Luther King worked for equality and he was a leader and his words would live forever. Gail murmured, "Maybe you'll grow up to be a leader." Tamara struggled to make sense of all the new things happening to her: Losing a tooth was a sign she was growing up. Her mother wanted her to be a leader like Martin Luther King and fight for equality. Maybe they wanted her words to live forever. Wide-eyed with excitement and a mixture of fear, Tamara blurted out, "But I'm not grown-up yet."

- Like to read about themselves.

    The world centers on five- and six-year-olds and they know it. They like books that celebrate their names, their wishes, their activities. They know they are the center of the universe and books that tell them so are just right.

- Like books that describe the world as they know it.

    Five and six year olds learn to count, say their ABCs, and write their names. They are assured that they are in charge of their world when their books confirm what they know. They like to rehearse their newfound knowledge by pointing to letters and numerals (numbers) in books.

Seven and Eight Year Olds

- Take pride in their ability to read.

    Seven and eight year olds are moving from assisted reading to independent reading. They take pleasure in demonstrating their skill at reading for any willing listener. They are as impressed as their listener. They will read almost anything that they are able to read.

- Read as a sometime thing.

    There are so many things going on in the seven- and eight-year-old's life that it's hard

The Reward

Lucy is paying her mother back. Anne spent endless hours reading to her. Now Lucy is a reader. She thinks books are the best gifts she receives. She entertains herself with a good book. She is into series, and because her grandparents took her to Colonial Williamsburg, Lucy devours the Samantha at Williamsburg series. One day, Lucy said, "Mom, I just read *Anne of Green Gables* and I think you'd like it, too." Lucy now recommends books to her mother.

to find time for reading. Electronic games dazzle their eyes. Bikes, baseball, soccer are important. They are very active, so we need to catch 'em on the run with short books, joke books, quick reads.

- Make friends a big priority.

    They most often choose friends of the same gender. They like books about people just like themselves who are true and loyal to a good friend.

- Think action is the name of the game.

    Shoot-'em-up television shows appeal to seven and eight year olds. Rough-and-tumble play is great. It doesn't matter much what game it is just so it moves. They like books about active characters who make things happen. They want things to happen in their books — no long, slow, descriptive paragraphs, please — just action.

- Strike out as independent people.

Seven and eight year olds are developing competence, a sense of self, and the desire to do things on their own. The amount of independence they can be allowed depends on a number of factors but their desire is to be in charge of themselves. They like books about children who go it alone, who are brave and independent. They choose their models from independent characters.

- Are able to understand more then they can read.

Seven and eight year olds can understand more complicated and complex stories when they hear them read aloud than when they read alone.

- Like the sharp line that distinguishes good and evil.

Sevens and eights want their good characters to be supremely good and don't like evil characters at all. They feel justified when evil is clearly trounced.

Animal Family

My ten-year-old grandson Jason loves anything with four legs. He helps out at a horse
stable in exchange for riding lessons. He has
a rabbit, Nibbles. He has a cat, Whiskers. He
has a dog, Gunner. Gunner was a three-pound
six-week-old tiny Labrador retriever puppy in
August when they brought him home. By De-
cember, Gunner was a forty-pound horse that
galloped over people (especially Grandma) and
furniture. If his parents would allow him to
have any more animals, he would have them.
Needless to say, Jason reads animal books.

Nine and Ten Year Olds

- Like animal books and poetry.
    Pets of any kind — horses, dogs, cats, —
    plus zoo animals, and make-believe animals
    appeal to readers this age.
- Like sports of all kinds.
    The active spirit continues. They play soccer,
    softball, basketball, football, or anything else
    they can throw or kick or catch. They read
    books about characters who do the same thing.
- Like funny books, joke books, humorous verse.
    When a nine or ten year old tells you a joke

they sometimes have to tell you when it's time to laugh, too. Even though their sense of humor is still developing, they can't seem to feed it enough. They devour books with anything funny in them.

- Develop a special interest.

    Nine and ten year olds start stamp collections, baseball card collections, rock collections, and butterfly collections. They play with computers, Nintendo, and Sega. They gather information through reading about their special interest. They want to read the *Guiness Book of World Records* and imagine seeing their own names in there someday.

- Like series books.

    It may be partly the collecting drive that causes nine and ten year olds to get every book in a series. They also take pride in reading every book in a series and compete with their friends to get the next one before they do.

- Listen to friends as much as family.

    Friends become very important. They find lots to do that interferes with reading; talking on the telephone to friends is one of the big items. They begin to dress like their friends, talk like their friends, and read what their friends read.

Eleven and Twelve Year Olds

- Are trying to find out who they are.

  They ask themselves: "Who am I?" and "What do I want to be?" Because they're going through such emotional upheavals they can be moody, temperamental, touchy, and quarrelsome. They like books about characters who are trying to figure out the same things they are. They want answers to questions, such as "What is life all about anyway?"

- Develop exclusive peer groups and cliques.

  They like secret clubs, clothes, hairstyles, or labels that show that they belong to a group. Groups become part of an extended family. They turn to groups for acceptance, support, and guidance. Books about characters who live in groups fascinate preteens.

- Show interest in the opposite sex.

  Girls read about romance, boys read science fiction, high fantasy, and adventure stories. They learn about how to relate to members of the opposite sex through books. They practice living up to their highest ideals through books.

- Are anxious to explore different life-styles.

  They want to see what it would be like to live a different life-style but they want to do it within the safe confines of their own home. That's part of the reason realistic "problem" books have such strong appeal.

Benjamin: Comic Book Collector

Eleven-year-old Ben collects comic books. Ben invests time, energy, and money: He keeps the comic books in shiny plastic covers that his two younger brothers dare not touch. Ben doesn't necessarily read the comic books, though, he just owns them.

Ben is an avid reader, however. He has read all of Roald Dahl's books and he reads adult books. Two books by Art Spiegelman, *Maus I* and *Maus II* written in cartoon style, held special fascination for Ben. When Ben heard that Spiegelman was coming to speak in his city, he insisted that his father get tickets.

Chapter 5:
Find Books to Meet
Your Child's Interests

Finding books for a child is one of the most pleasant tasks you will ever undertake. It's like looking for beautiful shells on the beach — there's always another more beautiful one just ahead. Here are some places to start looking.

Library

Talk to the librarians at the public library or school library. Their business is to know which books kids like. Their advice is priceless — and they have the books right there to hand to you. If they don't have the book, they will order it through interlibrary loan or perhaps purchase it if their budget permits.

Send a note to the librarian. Say, "We've looked for books on tarantulas and can't find any. Do you have any ideas where we could find out more about them?"

Look for new developments in book publishing, such as pop-up books and multiple path books. Pop-up books are masterful paper engineering that intrigue children and adults. You'll be fascinated as you unfold skyscrapers, planes, whole villages.

Many children like multiple path books. Children like being a part of the decision process — choosing what will happen next. They invariably read all the different possible paths.

Book Clubs

School Book Clubs. Some publishers and book distributors sell books through classrooms. Children receive an order form with descriptions of the books available; they choose the books they want to purchase.

Home and Mail Order Book Clubs. Several direct mail booksellers send descriptions of books to your home. You can join book clubs that are geared to your child's age level.

Bookstores and Toy Stores

Booksellers make a business of knowing which books kids like. Knowledgeable clerks in reputable stores know that if they sell you a really good book today that you'll be back for more next week or next month. They also know that you'll tell your neighbors and they will be in to buy books. It behooves them to know the best. Many grocery stores, novelty stores, discount stores, pharmacies, and houseware stores also carry children's books. You may need to look carefully at the offerings but there's no shortage of places to buy children's books.

Book Reviews

Children's books reviews appear in local, regional, and national newspapers. When you read a columnist for a while you know when you can trust her reviews and when you need to question them. Book reviews are a good way to keep up with new publications.

Children's Magazines

More than one hundred children's magazines are available — some are reviewed in *Read to Me*. Check the copies on the magazine shelf at your local library before you make the final selections for home delivery. The American Library Association as well as the Ed Press and International Reading Association have publications that review children's magazines. You can find these in your public library. (Addresses appear in the Appendix.)

Museum Shops

The child who likes art, science, or natural history and goes to museums will find books he wants to bring home. Museum shops are also a good place to find educational toys, games, and kits.

Book Fairs, Book Swaps

Some school parent organizations hold book fairs and/or book swaps. This is a good time to pick up new books at bargain prices. Have your child spend plenty of time exploring the display racks to make her list before you buy.

Booklists

People who work with children and books just love to make lists of things kids should read. We know that if we get a book on a list thousands of kids will get to enjoy it. (That's the way I feel about the lists in this book!)

Teachers create summer reading lists. Librarians develop reading club lists. Editors make a "best of the year" list. Committees in library organizations make a Notable Books list, a Best Books list, a list of Caldecott and Newbery award winners and honor books. Teachers conduct national field tests to discover Children's Choices,

Young Adult Choices, and Teachers' Choices. Ask your librarian if you could borrow some of the booklists to lead you to more good books.

Word of Mouth

The best advice comes from one person (satisfied consumer) to another. Talk with parents of your child's friends. Find out what other children are reading. Talk with your child's teacher and librarian. You may pick up ideas for books that really work.

Parenting Books

Parenting books (such as this one) always advise that we read aloud to children and they include lists of recommended books. They are a good source of information. Some favorite parenting books are listed in the Appendix.

Television Programs

There are some television programs, such as *Reading Rainbow*, that feature good children's books. Children like to read a book that they have seen featured in a film or video, so these programs are a good source for new books to read.

Chapter 6:
Moving Your Child
Along

Road sign on a back road in Vermont: Choose your rut carefully. You'll be in it for the next 40 miles.

At times, children get into a rut: They read the same things, eat the same things, wear the same things day after day. If your child is in a reading rut, you can move him out by helping him expand his interests. Here are a few ways to move him out.

Give Your Child Gifts

Choose your gifts wisely. Your child deserves

> (1) a library card
> (2) a few well-chosen books

(3) a book basket in the kitchen

(4) a bed lamp.

You are putting books in his path and making it easy for him to read them. If you talk about the books and show interest, your enthusiasm will be contagious.

Give books to your child for gifts. Birthdays, Christmas, Hanukkah, or any celebration is time for a book. One year, Ann and Tom noticed that Pam had not read the book they had given her last year so they wrapped it up again. Pam got the point — she read the book!

Plan special events with your child. Coordinate books with the activity. For example, if you plan a trip to the museum, go to the library to get some books on museum collections (art, history, anthropology). If you borrow the books and read them ahead of time, you'll get more out of the trip. If you read them after the visit, you'll extend the learning experience. Books help children continue to live in an experience longer.

Give your child the gift of respect. Let him read whatever interests him. No judgmental remarks about comic books, please. Noted author Jim Trelease says he had the biggest comic book collection in town. Instead of saying, "you can't read comic books," his parents let him read comics to his heart's content.

In the News

My granddaughter Kali gets very concerned about the homeless people she sees on the news. She and her parents have tracked down ways they can help by donating food and clothing but they have also found books such as Di Salvo's *Uncle Willie and the Soup Kitchen*, and Paula Fox's *Monkey Island*. The more Kali reads the better she will understand the problem and be able to help more effectively.

News items lead to reading. When your child watches the evening news with you, you are both exposed to many subjects that bear further investigation. Inauguarations lead to biographies of presidents and books about the political process. The Kentucky Derby leads to books about horses. The Super Bowl leads to books about football and biographies of football heroes. A local fire leads to books about firefighters. Follow up the news with a trip to the library.

What's Happening in School

School-related problems always bring a quick response from children who identify with them — or face them.

Twelve-year-old Kali is interested in anything about teenagers even though she isn't quite a teenager herself. Similar to all kids, she likes to read ahead of her age to see what life will be like. When she hears about teenagers using drugs or alcohol, teenage bulemia or anorexia, she talks about it at home. This is a perfect lead-in to books she reads avidly. She read Paula Fox's *The Moonlight Man* about an alcoholic father and Eve Bunting's story, *Jumping the Nail*, about teenage dares and dangerous challenges.

Share Your Own Interests

Children get interested in what we care about. When I was a young mother, I went back to college. Naturally I was interested in parenting, so I chose to study about the relation between what parents do with their children and the level of children's thinking.

After lots of home visits and interviews with parents, I concluded that children with the highest levels of creative thinking had parents who involved their children in their activities — whatever they happened to be. One mother was a competitive bowler and the whole family went along to keep score, read bowling magazines, and plan trips to other cities. One father was a gardener who had the whole family planning, pruning, and planting. One father was a woodworker. His children must have eaten tons of sawdust while they sanded wood and finished furniture. But they all learned from being with their parents.

Invite your child to participate in reading and writing you do at home:

add items to the grocery list
write notes on letters to relatives and friends
leave notes for parent who will be home late

Listen carefully to your children. You can pick up clues about their interests. I developed a shorthand way to talk about the study: "You get out of kids what you put into them — what you invest."

The chapters that follow arrange books by the readers' ages and interests. Like all booklists, these represent only a selection of the thousands of wonderful children's books that are available in bookstores and public libraries. We tried to mix all-time favorite titles with exciting new titles. To decide which interest categories to include, we listened to the questions children most often ask librarians and booksellers when they are looking for books to read for pleasure.

The titles listed here are jumping-off points. Let your children be your guides. They will let you know when a book is too difficult or too easy. Happy reading and happy sharing.

Chapter 7

Preschoolers

Things That Go, Things That Work

Barton, Byron. *Boats.* Illus. by author. HarperCollins, 1986. Bold colors and a simple text show sailboats, ferryboats, tugboats, and rowboats cutting through the water. Young children like to point and label each boat.

Barton, Byron. *Trucks.* Illus. by author. HarperCollins, 1986. Trucks do all sorts of work to help us live our daily lives. They carry building materials, garbage, gas and oil, among other things. Bold pictures show them at work.

Burton, Virginia Lee. *Mike Mulligan and His Steam Shovel.* Illus. by author. Houghton, 1939. There is always an important job for Mary Anne, the steam shovel. Man and machine are a match for any task, even when bigger, more powerful machines can't handle the job in this beloved story.

Gibbons, Gail. *Trucks*. Illus. by author. HarperCollins, 1981. Colorful drawings show trucks at work. Tank trucks, dump trucks, vendor trucks, fire trucks, and pick-up trucks are labeled.

Maestro, Betsy, and Ellen Del Vecchio. *Big City Port*. Illus. by Giulio Maestro. Scholastic, 1983. Action is everywhere down at the docks — on ships, trucks, ferries, ocean liners, and fireboats — on a busy day as cargo is unloaded and delivered all around the city.

Magee, Doug. *Trucks You Can Count On*. Illus. with photos. Putnam, 1985. Counting from one powerful engine to eighteen wheels leads young readers through a fascinating look at tractor trailer trucks.

Piper, Watty. *The Little Engine That Could*. Illus. by George and Doris Hauman. Platt & Munk, 1930. "I think I can — I think I can." This refrain inspires the little blue engine to try and to try harder until she pulls the train over the mountain to deliver toys to all the girls and boys.

Rockwell, Anne. *Bikes*. Illus. by author. Dutton, 1987. Playful tigers ride bicycles, tricycles, unicycles, tandem bikes, delivery bikes, exercise bikes, mopeds, and trail bikes. Fun for pointing and labeling.

Rockwell, Anne. *Big Wheels*. Illus. by author. Dutton, 1986. Vivid drawings of trucks, tractors, rollers, sweepers, cement mixers, snow-plows, and steam shovels fill the pages.

Rockwell, Anne. *Planes*. Illus. by author. Dutton, 1985. Come aboard all different types of aircraft, from homemade models to modern jets, and take a flight with the crew. Simple, uncluttered drawings are used to show how people and cargo move through the air.

Rockwell, Anne. *Trucks*. Illus. by author. Dutton, 1984. Fifteen types of trucks include snow plow, garbage truck, moving van, camper, ice cream truck, and more.

Smath, Jerry. *Wheels on the Bus*. Grosset & Dunlap, 1991. There's lots of action on the bus as babies cry, dogs bark, and the horn goes beep. This board book is just the right size for small hands to hold as they sing the words to the familiar nursery song.

ABC Books

Anno, Mitsumasa. *Anno's Alphabet*. Illus. by author. Crowell, 1976. Play a game of hide-and-seek with the alphabet. Preschoolers love to search the pictures and name the objects beginning with the same letter.

Aylesworth, Jim. *Old Black Fly*. Illus. by Stephen Gammell. Holt, 1992. A bothersome fly disrupts the household as it lights on things in alphabetical order from A to Z. Perfect for chanting aloud.

Azarian, Mary. *Farmer's Alphabet*. Illus. by author. Godine, 1981. In a truly remarkable book, striking woodcuts appear in black and white and are set off by letters and a word set in red.

Blake, Quentin. *Quentin Blake's ABC*. Illus. by author. Knopf, 1989. A deceptively simple rhyming text sets off Blake's humorous illustrations for each letter of the alphabet.

De Brunhoff, Laurent. *Babar's ABC*. Illus. by author. Random House, 1983. Characters from Celesteville illustrate each letter of the alphabet.

Demi. *Demi's Find the Animal A B C: An Alphabet Game Book*. Illus. by author. Grosset & Dunlap, 1985. A beautifully designed find-the-animal game arranged in alphabetical order.

Feelings, Muriel. *Jambo Means Hello: Swahili Alphabet Book*. Illus. by Tom Feelings. Dial, 1974. Each of the letters of the Swahili alphabet is exquisitely illustrated with items from the Swahili culture.

Geisert, Arthur. *Pigs from A to Z*. Illus. by author. Houghton, 1986. Seven pigs build a tree house fitting in alphabetical arrangement.

Hague, Kathleen. *Alphabears: An ABC Book*. Illus. by Michael Hague. Holt, 1984. Twenty-six huggable teddy bears introduce themselves and tell what they like to do in simple rhymes.

Hoban, Tana. *A B See*. Black & white photograms. Greenwillow, 1982. Photograms of familiar objects intrigue children who will want to label them. Some may require an adult's help.

Hoban, Tana. *26 Letters and 99 Cents*. Color photographs. Greenwillow, 1987. A combined alphabet and counting book.

Hoguet, Susan Ramsay. *I Unpacked My Grandmother's Trunk: A Picture Book Game*. Illus. by author. Dutton, 1983. Play the memory game as you add another item to the trunk.

Kitchen, Bert. *Animal Alphabet*. Illus. by author. Dial, 1984. Guess the names of the beautifully illustrated animals.

Lionni, Leo. *Alphabet Tree*. Illus. by author. Knopf, 1990. A fuzzy purple caterpillar teaches words how to get together to create a special message.

Lobel, Anita. *Alison's Zinnia*. Illus. by author. Greenwillow, 1990. Amy has an Amaryllis and Zena has a Zinnia. In between all the girls are matched with a flower beginning with the same letter as their name.

Lobel, Arnold. *On Market Street*. Illus. by Anita Lobel. Greenwillow, 1981. A young boy goes shopping on a street filled with people who are made from the objects they sell.

MacDonald, Suse. *Alphabatics*. Illus. by author. Bradbury, 1986. Each letter of the alphabet turns into an object beginning with that letter.

Martin, Bill, Jr., and John Archambault. *Chicka Chicka Boom Boom*. Illus. by Lois Ehlert. Simon & Schuster, 1989. The predictable phrase, meet you at the top of the coconut tree, underscores the rap beat of A told B and B told C.

Sendak, Maurice. *Alligators All Around: An Alphabet*. Illus. by author. HarperCollins, 1962. Only Sendak could create so much subtle humor and downright child's play in an alphabet book.

Seuss, Dr. *Dr. Seuss's ABC*. Illus. by author. Random House, 1963. Colorful pages filled with zany Seuss characters bouncing about on the alphabet.

Count to Ten, Then Again

Fleming, Denise. *Count!* Illus. by author. Holt, 1992. Familiar animals are available to be counted, but they have to hold still as children count from 1 to 10 and 20, 30, 40, and 50 as well.

Jones, Carol, compiler. *This Old Man*. Illus. by the compiler. Houghton, 1990. Where will the old man play nicknack next? Children look through the peephole on each page to find the answer as they count along with this traditional song.

Langstaff, John, compiler. *Over In The Meadow*. Illus. by Feodor Rojankovsky. HB, 1957. Meet all the baby animals and their mothers who live in the meadow in this well-known counting song.

Sis, Peter. *Going Up! A Color Counting Book*. Illus. by author. Greenwillow, 1989. Colors and numbers are the clues to solving an exciting story that delights young children.

Young, Ed. *Seven Blind Mice*. Illus. by author. Philomel, 1992. Preschoolers enjoy the humor of each mouse trying to guess the elephant's identity by feeling just a small part of its body. Naming the shapes, colors, and days of the week contribute to the fun of reading this book.

Lift the Flap, Toy Books

Ahlberg, Janet and Allan. *The Jolly Postman and Other People's Letters*. Illus. by authors. Little, Brown, 1986. The Postman delivers letters from one Mother Goose character to another. The hard part will be keeping the tiny notes, postcards, and letters in the right spot.

Dijs, Carla. *Are You My Mommy?* Illus. by author. Simon & Schuster, 1990. Baby chick has just hatched and is looking for her mommy in this pop-up book. Each animal mother describes herself and what she says until mother and baby are reunited.

Hawkins, Colin, and Jacqui Hawkins. *Old Mother Hubbard.* Putnam, 1985. Lift the flaps and open the cupboard doors to find out what silly thing is going to happen next to Old Mother Hubbard and her faithful dog. Cartoon illustrations give this old story a modern feeling.

Hill, Eric. *Where's Spot?* Illus. by author. Putnam, 1980. Lift the flaps to help Spot's mother find where Spot is hiding. Preschoolers love opening doors and lifting flaps in a series of books featuring the puppy, Spot. Some other titles are: *Spot at Play, Spot on the Farm,* and *Spot Goes to the Circus.*

Wijngaard, Juan. *Bear.* Illus. by author. Crown, 1991. One in a series of board books featuring familiar animals playing with everyday objects. A fine choice for lap reading.

Poetry and Mother Goose Rhymes

Dalton, Anne. *This Is the Way.* Illus. by author. Scholastic, 1992. Sing your way through the day's activities with a cozy, loving family whose routine will be familiar to preschoolers.

Delacre, Lulu, selector. *Arroz Con Leche: Popular Songs and Rhymes from Latin America.* Illus. by selector. Scholastic, 1989. English and Spanish versions of well-known Latin American songs that celebrate Spanish culture.

Foreman, Michael, editor. *Michael Foreman's Mother Goose.* Illus. by editor. HB, 1991. All the familiar nursery rhymes are here in a book just the right size for sharing with a preschooler on your lap. Sometimes the nursery rhyme characters appear in the next illustration, like an old friend come to visit.

Galdone, Paul, adapter. *Three Little Kittens.* Illus. by adapter. Clarion, 1986. The three little kittens look just as sad as any children who have ever lost their mittens and just as joyous when kittens and mittens are reunited in this well-known poem.

Sharon, Lois & Bram's Mother Goose: Songs, Finger Rhymes, Tickling Verses, Games & More. Illus. by Maryann Kovalski. Little, Brown/Joy Street, 1986. The title says it all, there are hours of amusement here for the youngest audience.

Hopkins, Lee Bennett, compiler. *Side By Side: Poems To Read Together.* Illus. by Hilary Knight. Simon & Schuster, 1988. The invitation is to snuggle comfortably with your child and read together — poems by favorite authors as well as traditional alphabet songs, counting rhymes, finger plays, and nursery rhymes.

Langstaff, John. *Frog Went A-Courtin'*. Illus. by Feodor Rojankovsky. HB, 1955. Mr. Frog is all dressed up with his sword and pistol by his side to win the hand of Miss Mouse in this old ballad sung by the early colonists and still popular.

Mattox, Cheryl Warren. *Shake It to the One That You Love the Best: Play Songs and Lullabies from Black Musical Traditions*. Illus. by Varnette Honeywood and Brenda Joysmith. Warren-Mattox Productions, 1989. A rich collection of twenty-six songs reflecting optimism, friendship, and hopefulness as sung in the African-American community.

Stevens, Janet, adapter. *The House That Jack Built*. Illus. by adapter. Holiday, 1985. As the rhyme repeats itself and adds on a cast of busy characters, the tiny pictures illustrating each line are repeated so that preschoolers can "read" the story, too.

Spier, Peter, adapter, *London Bridge Is Falling Down*. Illus. by adapter. Doubleday, 1972. A perennial favorite song and simple game for preschoolers, illustrated with traditional pictures of England from another era.

Theobalds, Prue, adapter. *Old MacDonald Had a Farm*. Illus. by adapter. Peter Bedrick, 1991. Showing the changing seasons and activities on the farm, this new version of favorite circle game calls for frequent retellings.

Weiss, Nicki, editor. *If You're Happy and You Know It: Eighteen Story Songs Set to Pictures*. Greenwillow, 1987. The songs are well-known old favorites, just right for the nursery school set, the pictures are stories that lend themselves to reading.

Westcott, Nadine Bernard, adapter. *I Know an Old Lady Who Swallowed a Fly*. Illus. by adapter. Little, Brown/Joy Street, 1980. A hilarious adaptation in words and illustrations sure to tickle the imaginations of preschoolers.

Westcott, Nadine Bernard, adapter. *Skip to My Lou*. Illus. by adapter. Little, Brown/Joy Street, 1989. Humorous drawings portray the comic adventures of a little boy left in charge of the family farm as the words to the song are sung.

Yolen, Jane, editor. *The Lap-Time Song and Play Book*. Illus. by Margot Tomes. HB, 1989. With your preschooler on your lap, play the finger games you remember from your own childhood: "Eensy, Weensy Spider," "Pat-a-Cake," and other familiar songs. Each song has playing instructions and musical arrangements.

Apple, Margot. *Blanket*. Illus. by author. Houghton, 1990. A small child fears Blanket will be sad out on the clothesline overnight and can't fall asleep for worrying about Blanket. The clothes, the dog, the cat, and the wind work together to reunite Blanket and child for a good night's sleep.

Asch, Frank. *Happy Birthday, Moon*. Illus. by author. Prentice-Hall, 1982. Bear decides to give his friend, the moon, a birthday present. He chooses carefully and, like a good friend, is forgiving when moon apologizes for losing his beautiful birthday hat.

Brown, Margaret Wise. *The Runaway Bunny*. Illus. by Clement Hurd. HarperCollins, 1942. No matter how he plans to run away, mother bunny reassures her runaway bunny that she will find him and protect him until he's safe at home again.

Cazet, Denys. *I'm Not Sleepy*. Illus. by author. Orchard, 1992. Despite his protests that he's not really sleepy, Alex's father is sure a bedtime story is just what Alex needs.

Ginsburg, Mirra. *Asleep, Asleep*. Illus. by Nancy Tafuri. Greenwillow, 1992. The whole world is asleep except you and the wind, a mother sings quietly to her baby. A simple, repetitive lullaby sure to induce sleep in the most reluctant young child. The illustrations reflect a calm scene of peace and quiet.

Hayes, Sarah. *This Is the Bear and the Scary Night*. Illus. by Helen Craig. Little, Brown/Joy Street, 1992. A stuffed bear is left behind in the park and, after a series of scary adventures, is reunited with his owner.

Marshall, James. *George and Martha*. Illus. by author. Houghton, 1972. Friendship carries the day as these best friend hippos learn to care about each other's feelings.

Pilkey, Dav. *When Cats Dream*. Illus. by author. Orchard, 1992. Nestled on a warm snuggly lap, cats dream in bright technicolor compared to the drab gray of their daytime existence.

Titherington, Jeanne, adapter. *Baby's Boat*. Illus. by adapter. Greenwillow, 1992. A traditional lullaby pictures baby sailing off to sleep among the stars with a teddy bear for company. Pastel illustrations in purple and lavender are soothing and dreamlike.

Waddell, Martin. *Can't You Sleep, Little Bear?* Illus. by Barbara Firth. Candlewick, 1992. Little Bear is afraid of the dark and nothing reassures him until Big Bear carries him outside to see the bright moon and shining stars.

Wells, Rosemary. *Max's Birthday*. Illus. by author. Dial, 1985. Max the bunny is excited about opening a birthday present from his sister, Ruby, and then scared by the dragon he finds inside. This is one of several books that describe Max's efforts to behave like a big bunny.

Colors

Brown, Margaret Wise. *Red Light, Green Light*. Illus. by Leonard Weisgard. Scholastic, 1992. Originally published in 1945, the new edition still tells the story of traffic lights and their Stop and Go message.

Dodds, Dayle Ann. *The Color Box*. Illus. by Giles Laroche. Little, Brown, 1992. Alexander, a small monkey, crawls into a magic box to the land of yellow and other spots of color.

Ehlert, Lois. *Planting a Rainbow*. Illus. by author. HarperCollins, 1988. Together mother and child work to plant a garden: bulbs in the fall and seeds in the spring. Together they gather their rainbow of brilliant primary colored flowers.

Fleming, Denise. *Lunch*. Illus. by author. Holt, 1992. A hungry mouse eats his way through brightly colored fruits and vegetables.

Freeman, Don. *The Chalk Box*. Illus. by author. HarperCollins, 1976. Children identify pieces of colored chalk to help rescue a boy stranded on an island he has drawn with the chalk.

Greeley, Valerie. *White Is the Moon*. Illus. by author. Macmillan, 1991. Simple, short poems introduce a different animal and color on each page.

Hoban, Tana. *Is It Larger? Is It Smaller?* Photos by the author. Greenwillow, 1985. Colorful photographs of familiar animals and objects are shown to illustrate the concept of size in this wordless picture book.

Jonas, Ann. *Color Dance.* Illus. by author. Greenwillow, 1989. Colors combine to make new colors when young children dance, waving gauzy scarves as they twirl and whirl through the air.

Martin, Bill, Jr. *Brown Bear, Brown Bear, What Do You See?* Illus. by Eric Carle. Holt, 1983. As you chant the first part of the verse, your preschooler will respond with the verse that names a familiar animal and a crayon bright color.

Sawicki, Norma J. *The Little Red House.* Illus. by Toni Goffe. Lothrop, 1989. As a set of nesting houses is uncovered, a child discovers each house is a different color waiting to be named.

Families

Abercrombie, Barbara. *Charlie Anderson.* Illus. by Mark Graham. Macmillan, 1990. Two sisters, whose parents are divorced, discover that their cat has a second home, just like they do.

Ackerman, Karen. *Song and Dance Man*. Illus. by Stephen Gammell. Knopf, 1988. Three children visit Grandpa, who performs his old vaudeville act for them.

Adoff, Arnold, *Black Is Brown Is Tan*. Illus. by Emily Arnold McCully. HarperCollins, 1973. A multiracial family as they work, play, sing, tease, and love each other.

Ahlberg, Janet. *Baby's Catalogue*. Illus. by Janet and Allan Ahlberg. Little, Brown, 1982. All the familiar objects that six babies need — food, equipment, clothing, toys, and pets. Children want to point to and label each item.

Aliki. *Two of Them*. Illus. by author. Greenwillow, 1979. A grandfather spends lots of time taking care of and doing things for his little granddaughter. When he grows old, she takes care of him.

Carlstrom, Nancy White. *How Do You Say It Today, Jesse Bear?* Illus. by Bruce Degen. Macmillan, 1992. Jesse Bear finds so many ways to show how much he loves his mother all through the year until he says "I love you!"

Gill, Madeline. *The Spring Hat*. Illus. by author. Simon & Schuster, 1993. Baby bunnies use Mama Bunny's hat as a frisbee while she naps. It floats away in the river and they collect flowers to make her a new hat in this wordless picture book.

Hughes, Shirley. *The Big Alfie Out of Doors Storybook*. Illus. by author. Lothrop, 1992. Four charming stories about Alfie, his family, and his stuffed animals. Perfect for laptime story reading.

Lacoe, Addie. *Just Not the Same*. Houghton, 1992. Triplets Cleo, Mirabelle, and Gertrude learn that sharing doesn't always mean exactly equal in a series of hilarious sharing experiences.

Mora, Pat. *A Birthday Basket for Tia*. Illus. by Cecily Lang. Macmillan, 1992. Cecilia creates a special present for her great-aunt's 90th birthday, a basket of memories representing special times and favorite activities they've shared.

Waddell, Martin. *Sam Vole and His Brothers*. Candlewick, 1992. Sam Vole, a young field mouse, wants to do something on his own. When he goes out alone one morning he discovers how nice it is to have his brothers around after all.

The Wide, Wide World

Ballard, Robin. *My Father Is Far Away*. Greenwillow, 1992. A little girl misses her father and imagines him hurrying back to her, missing her, too, even in the midst of his exciting adventures.

Brooke, L. Leslie. *The Golden Goose Book: A Fairy Tale Picture Book*. Clarion, 1992. Four favorite fairy tales as told nearly a century ago. The original illustrations are alive with animation and excitement sure to please children.

Brown, Ruth. *The Picnic*. Illus. by author. Dutton, 1992. In a reversal of roles, people invade the animals' picnic, sending them scurrying for cover. Rain arrives, chasing the people and leaving a great feast for the animals.

Carlstrom, Nancy White. *The Snow Speaks*. Illus. by Jane Dyer. Little, Brown, 1992. Share the experience of a snowstorm in the country with a brother and sister, catch the first flakes, and then play in the snow.

Hennessy, B. G. *The Missing Tarts*. Illus. by Tracey Campbell Pearson. Viking Kestrel, 1989. The familiar nursery rhyme has been hilariously updated. As the queen gives chase she is joined by Jack and Jill and other nursery characters.

Hines, Anna Grossnickle. *Rumble, Tumble Boom!* Greenwillow, 1992. A father comforts his son during a nighttime thunderstorm with the explanation that it's just the "air bumping into itself" as the whole family snuggles in bed together.

Rotner, Shelley, and Ken Kreisler. *Nature Spy*. Photos by Shelley Rotner. Macmillan, 1992. Through a series of photos that move ever closer to the subject, nature's colors are seen as bright and sparkling, inviting children outdoors to see for themselves.

Shaw, Nancy. *Sheep Out to Eat*. Illus. by Margot Apple. Houghton, 1992. Oh! what a mess these sheep make as they really try their best to eat neatly. The rhymed verse captures the madcap humor of the situation.

Sis, Peter. *An Ocean World*. Greenwillow, 1992. A small whale grows too big for his tank and is released into the sea where he begins his search for another whale. He approaches a submarine, an island, and a barge until he meets another whale.

Voake, Charlotte, selector. *Three Little Pigs and Other Favorite Nursery Stories*. Illus. by selector. Candlewick, 1992. Ten well-known nursery stories delight preschoolers, especially the title story and "The Gingerbread Boy."

Wood, Don and Audrey Wood. *Piggies*. Illus. by Don Wood. HB, 1991. Small piggy puppets fit on the fingertips of a small child in this variation of the traditional "this little piggy game" offering a new opportunity for parent and child play.

Chapter 8

Five and Six Year Olds

Dinosaurs

Aliki. *Digging Up Dinosaurs*. Illus. by author. Crowell, 1981. The excitement of reconstructing a dinosaur skeleton and putting together a museum exhibit is told in word and picture. Behind-the-scenes work is as much fun as digging up dinosaur bones.

Blumenthal, Nancy. *Count-a-saurus*. Illus. by Robert Jay Kaufman. Macmillan, 1989. Travel back to prehistoric times and count ten prehistoric dinosaurs. An append-a-saurus at the back of the book briefly tells about each creature.

Hoff, Syd. *Danny and the Dinosaur*. Illus. by author. HarperCollins, 1958, 1986. An I Can Read Book that's a perennial favorite when children ask for a dinosaur story. Danny visits a museum where a friendly dinosaur offers to go home and play with Danny and his friends for a day.

Gibbons, Gail. *Dinosaurs.* Illus. by author. Holiday, 1987. Bold, bright illustrations make dinosaurs easy to identify. Dinosaur names and a key to pronunciation accompany each illustration along with a few short sentences.

Most, Bernard. *Happy Hollidaysaurus!* Illus. by author. HB, 1992. Dinosaurs are used to highlight various holidays renamed Arborsaurus Day and Eastersaurus. On May Day it is brachiosaurus with his long neck who performs as the maypole. Light and humorous depiction of several dinosaur species.

Mullin, Patricia. *Dinosaur Encore.* Harper-Collins, 1993. Fold-out double-page spreads compare dinosaurs with living animals, letting readers see the difference in size. Questions about dinosaurs appear throughout the book, giving children a chance to think like scientists.

Osborne, Mary Pope. *Dinosaurs Before Dark.* Illus. by Sal Murdocca. Random House, 1992. A brother and sister travel back in time 65 million years. They meet several species of dinosaurs and deal with erupting volcanoes before returning home safely.

Prelutsky, Jack. *Tyrannosaurus Was a Beast: Dinosaur Poems.* Illus. by Arnold Lobel. Greenwillow, 1988. A collection of fourteen humorous poems about different species of dinosaurs. The humorous verses and their illustrations explain how each one lived, what it ate, and how it looked.

Simon, Seymour. *The Largest Dinosaurs.* Illus. by Pamela Carroll. Macmillan, 1986. Describes the biggest species of dinosaurs and discusses the clues used by scientists to help explain their disappearance. A companion title by Simon is *The Smallest Dinosaurs.*

Sirois, Allen L. *Dinosaurs Dress Up.* Illus. by Janet Street. Morrow, 1992. A silly story pretending to explain why dinosaurs became extinct. Dinosaurs loved to dress up but would argue fiercely about what was fashionable, tearing each other's clothes off. An absurd extended joke with great child appeal.

Sweat, Lynn, and Louis Phillips. *The Smallest Stegosaurus.* Illus. by Lynn Sweat. Viking, 1993. A young stegosaurus wants to help, but what is there for a small dinosaur to do? When a new baby sister arrives opportunities to be helpful occur in this picture book. The dinosaurs are accurately drawn.

Families and Friends

De Brunhoff, Laurent. *Babar's Family Album.* Illus. by author. Random House, 1991. A perennial favorite, stories of Babar and his family are timeless treasures for each new generation. Five stories are published in one volume, sure to please fans who can never get enough of the elephant family's adventures.

Delaney, Molly. *My Sister.* Illus. by author. Atheneum, 1989. After listing all the things her big sister doesn't do for her, a younger sister lovingly reminds herself that when she's scared at night it's her big sister who takes her into bed and comforts her.

Everitt, Betsy. *Mean Soup.* HB, 1992. Horace has a terrible day at school so Mom helps him boil water and throw all his mean and nasty thoughts into the soup pot until Horace is smiling again.

Fox, Mem. *Wilfrid Gordon McDonald Partridge.* Illus. by Julie Vivas. Kane/Miller, 1984. Wilfrid Gordon searches all over to find the meaning of "memory" so he can help his friend Miss Nancy who lives next door at the old people's home find hers.

Kraus, Robert. *Leo the Late Bloomer.* Illus. by Jose Aruego. Windmill, 1971. Leo's father keeps watching for signs of big tiger behavior from Leo. Children cheer when Leo blooms in his own good time as a reader, writer, and speaker.

Lobel, Arnold. *Frog and Toad Are Friends.* Illus. by author. HarperCollins, 1970. Best friends are always there to help each other as frog and toad demonstrate in five stories in this easy to read storybook.

Minarik, Else Holmelund. *Little Bear*. Illus. by Maurice Sendak. HarperCollins, 1957. Little Bear is encouraged to try new adventures because Mother Bear is always waiting at home with a reassuring hug and kiss in this classic easy to read book.

Numeroff, Laura Joffe. *If You Give a Moose a Muffin*. Illus. by Felicia Bond. HarperCollins, 1991. A comical sequence of events is set in motion when a boy throws a muffin to his friend, a moose. Each action sets off its own reaction in not quite logical succession, just as in the author's *If You Give a Mouse a Cookie*.

Polacco, Patricia. *Mrs. Katz and Tush*. Illus. by author. Bantam, 1992. Larnel, an African-American boy brings Mrs. Katz, an elderly Jewish woman, a tailless kitten she names Tush. He listens to her stories of earlier times and they play with the kitten as a strong bond of friendship develops between them.

Ringgold, Faith. *Tar Beach*. Illus. by author. Crown, 1991. Cassie dreams of flying over the rooftops of her Harlem neighborhood as she learns how to let her imagination take flight and set her free on a starry summer night.

Sawyer, Ruth. *Journey Cake, Ho!* Illus. by Robert McCloskey. Viking, 1953. A southern version of the Gingerbread Boy, Johnny chases the Journey Cake until they come full circle back to the farm where the farmer and his wife welcome Johnny, the missing animals, and the singing Journey Cake.

Sendak, Maurice. *Where the Wild Things Are.* Illus. by author. HarperCollins, 1963. Max can go home again, he can return from where the wild things are in his dreams because his mother loves him no matter what and will be waiting with a hot dinner for him.

Snyder, Diane. *The Boy of the Three Year Nap.* Illus. by Allan Say. Houghton, 1988. To the despair of his mother and the delight of readers, Taro manages to win a beautiful wife and great wealth without having to work for them. In fact, he seems to spend all his time being lazy and sleeping.

Steig, William. *Doctor DeSoto Goes to Africa.* Illus. by author. HarperCollins, 1992. Fans of the first Doctor DeSoto story will delight in this new title. The good mouse dentist hurries off to Africa when an elephant complains of a toothache and is kidnapped, setting off a chain of improbable events.

Wood, Audrey. *King Bidgood's in the Bathtub.* Illus. by Don Wood. HB, 1985. The king never likes to get out of the bathtub and rule his kingdom in proper fashion. Finally, a young page supplies the solution — pull the plug. Deliciously funny illustrations and a predictable text invite beginning readers to "read along."

Yolen, Jane. *Owl Moon.* Illus. by John Schoenherr. Philomel, 1987. On a quiet winter evening a father and daughter go for a quiet walk in the woods hoping to see an owl. The striking illustrations of father and daughter are memorable.

New Babies

Baker, Jeannie. *Window.* Illus. by author. Greenwillow, 1991. Sam's mother holds him up as she looks through his nursery window at the countryside. As he changes and grows, the scene outside changes and grows, too.

Brown, Laurie Krasny. *Baby Time.* Illus. by Marc Brown. Knopf, 1989. For all big brothers and sisters, a book to help them learn to take care of the new baby in the family. It's a baby-care book that explains how babies develop and what to do to keep them safe and happy.

Frazier, Debra. *On the Day You Were Born.* Illus. by author. HB, 1991. The whole world is on hand to greet the birth of a new baby. Paper collages convey a sense of wonder and welcome as word of the birth is passed among the animals and elements in the universe.

Henkes, Kevin. *Julius, the Baby of the World.* Illus. by author. Greenwillow, 1990. Lilly is an unhappy big sister; her parents adore everything the baby does. When Lilly does the same things, she has to sit in her chair. When a cousin criticizes Julius, Lilly defends him, realizing how much she loves him.

Holabird, Katharine. *Angelina's Baby Sister.* Illus. by Craig Helen. Clarkson Potter, 1991. Angelina mouse has a temper tantrum when new baby Polly gets all the attention. With the reassurance of her family, Angelina promises to share her love of ballet dancing with Polly when she gets big.

Keats, Ezra Jack. *Peter's Chair.* Illus. by author. HarperCollins, 1967. Peter is upset and runs away when he sees his crib, cradle, and high chair painted pink for the new baby until he realizes how important it is to be the big brother.

Lasky, Kathryn. *A Baby for Max.* Photos by Christopher Knight. Scribner's, 1984. With photos taken by his father and a story written by his mother, five-year-old Max tells how he feels about becoming a big brother.

Matthews, Downs. *Polar Bear Cubs.* Illus. by Dan Guravich. Simon & Schuster, 1989. A mother polar bear feeds her two cubs and keeps them safe and warm over the course of an arctic year. The mother's devotion to her cubs as they learn to walk on ice, hunt, and fish are revealed in a stunning photographic essay.

McCloskey, Robert. *Make Way for Ducklings.* Illus. by author. Viking, 1941. Mother duck safely shepherds her new baby ducklings across Boston Common. There is comfort and reassurance in Mrs. Mallard doing naturally what all mothers do.

ABC and Counting Books

Agard, John. *The Calypso Alphabet.* Illus. by Jennifer Bent. Holt, 1989. Learn the alphabet to the gentle rhythm of a Calypso beat. Simple rhymes and island scenes depict the flavor of daily life in the Caribbean.

Aylesworth, Jim. *The Folks in the Valley: A Pennsylvania Dutch ABC.* Illus. by Stefano Vitale. HarperCollins, 1992. Rural scenes celebrate quiet contentment and strong family bonds of the Pennsylvania Dutch community in this rhyming alphabet book.

Garne, S. T. *One White Sail: A Caribbean Counting Book.* Illus. by Lisa Etre. Simon & Schuster, 1992. Bright colors and lilting island rhythms capture the flavor of the Caribbean in a counting book featuring palm trees and steel drums.

Giganti, Paul. *Each Orange Had Eight Slices.* Illus. by Donald Crews. Greenwillow, 1992. Each double-page spread offers a chance to count the items pictured or see them as a related set and add or multiply them. Bold graphic illustrations encourage reader participation.

Grossman, Virginia. *Ten Little Rabbits.* Illus. by Sylvia Long. Chronicle Books, 1991. Rabbits from one to ten perform traditional Native American customs and chores on double-page spreads in earth tones. Notes at the back help readers identify each tribe that is represented.

Gustafson, Scott. *Alphabet Soup: A Feast of Letters.* Illus. by author. Calico Bks, 1990. Otter finds a big soup pot in his house and invites 26 friends to come for a pot luck supper. Armadillo brings asparagus, koala brings kumquats and krill, and the feast is prepared.

Hepworth, Cathi. *ANTics! An Alphabetical Anthology.* Illus. by author. Putnam, 1992. Santa is a tiny ant wearing a Santa suit, pulling a heavy bag of toys; 26 ants from A to Z do all manner of fantastic things explained by a one-word description.

Hoban, Tana. *Spirals, Curves, Fanshapes, and Lines.* Greenwillow, 1992. Birthday cakes and candles, spaghetti and doorways all have their own shapes. This wordless picture book introduces the concept of shapes through photographs of everyday objects.

Johnson, Bruce, and Odette. *Apples, Alligators, and Also Alphabets.* Illus. by authors. Oxford, 1991. Lots of amusing details and a sense of texture to the artwork makes this book special. The illustration for each letter shows many items for beginning readers to identify.

Magee, Darcy, and Robert Newman. *Let's Fly From A to Z.* Cobblehill, 1992. Fly along in the cockpit of a sleek jet plane or sit in the control tower of a busy airport as the activities and equipment necessary to keep the big jets flying are explained.

McMillan, Bruce. *One Two, One Pair!* Photos by author. Scholastic, 1991. Beyond simple counting is the concept of pairs of things. Bright photos illustrate many examples of everyday objects that come in pairs.

Marzollo, Jean. *I Spy: A Book of Picture Riddles.* Photos by Walter Wick. Scholastic, 1992. Play along and identify the objects named in rhyming riddles on each double-page spread. At the end of the book young readers are given a chance to make up their own riddles.

Ryden, Hope. *Wild Animals of Africa ABC.* Photos by author. Dutton, 1989. Many of the animals are unfamiliar — what's a xoxo? Large color photos of the animals are accompanied by the name of the animal and the letter of the alphabet. Descriptions of the animals are given at the end of the book.

Walsh, Ellen Stoll. *Mouse Count.* Illus. by author. HB, 1991. A sneaky snake slithers off to find the eleventh mouse to add to his meal while the first ten mice escape from the jar, counting themselves down to one as they go.

Van Allsburg, Chris. *The Z Was Zapped.* Illus. by author. Houghton, 1987. Come to the theater where the letters of the alphabet are the star performers. Each letter gets a chance to play a major role and tell something about itself.

Poetry and Song

Belloc, Hilaire. *Matilda, Who Told Lies, And Was Burned to Death.* Illus. by Posy Simmonds. Knopf, 1992. Matilda, a fiendish looking child, turns in a false alarm to the London Fire Brigade one too many times. Children will laugh at the wicked smile on Matilda's face as she works her evil and then gets her comeuppance.

Clark, Emma Chichester, selector. *I Never Saw a Purple Cow and Other Nonsense Rhymes.*

Illus. by selector. Little, Brown, 1991. British limericks, jump-rope rhymes, and song lyrics are simply silly and fun to recite. Some are new, some are novel, offering a glimpse at what makes other children giggle.

Field, Eugene. *The Gingham Dog and the Calico Cat.* Illus. by Janet Street. Philomel, 1990. The gingham dog and the calico cat, stuffed animals in a toy shop, get into a furious fight with bits and pieces of gingham and calico flying all over till not a trace of them remains.

Guthrie, Woody. *Woody's 20 Grow Big Songs.* Illus. by author. HarperCollins, 1992. Twenty previously unpublished songs from this famous folksinger burst with energy and action. Many of the songs have repetitive verses and easy to sing melodies. A recording by Arlo Guthrie of the songs is available.

Hawkes, Kevin. *Then the Troll Heard the Squeak.* Illus. by author. Lothrop, 1991. Little Miss Terry jumps on her bed in the middle of the night sending grandma's false teeth flying and waking the troll in the basement who comes to teach her a funny lesson.

Kennedy, Dorothy & X.J., selectors. *Talking Like the Rain: A First Book of Poems.* Illus. by Jane Dyer. Little, Brown, 1992. Another superb collection from this pair of master anthologists. Nine sections organized by themes familiar to young readers present a selection of well-known children's poets.

Kennedy, Jimmy, lyrics. *The Teddy Bears' Picnic.* Music by John Bratton. Illus. by Renate Kozikowski. Aladdin, 1989. Dance and sing along with the teddy bears as they go to the woods for their annual picnic and day of games. Turn the cut-out half pages to reveal the festive goings-on.

Kuskin, Karla. *Soap Soup and Other Verses.* HarperCollins, 1992. An easy-to-read book of lighthearted poems about the everyday world of children. With warmth and humor readers are offered a fresh view of familiar scenes.

Larrick, Nancy, compiler. *Mice Are Nice.* Illus. by Ed Young. Philomel, 1990. Twenty-five poems describe mice in all their settings. Readers see mice scampering outdoors and twitching their whiskers indoors when they sense trouble. Here they are always fun-loving furry creatures who love to play.

Lee, Dennis. *The Ice Cream Store.* Illus. by David McPhail. Scholastic, 1992. A collection of nonsense poems that takes delight in the diversity of children. The title poem refers to the variety of children living in the neighborhood, other poems celebrate those children and their emotions with warmth and humor.

Livingston, Myra Cohn. *Birthday Poems.* Illus. by Margot Tomes. Holiday, 1989. Twenty-four poems about youngsters' favorite subject — their own birthdays. The poems are short and upbeat, celebrating birthdays.

Moore, Lilian. *Adam Mouse's Book of Poems.* Illus. by Kathleen Garry McCord. Atheneum, 1992. Readers share the author's delight in the natural world and all living creatures. Simple language conveys a delightful sense of sound and imagery.

Stevenson, Robert Louis. *My Shadow.* Illus. by Ted Rand. Putnam, 1990. A beloved poem with illustrations showing children playing all over the world and how their shadows play right along with them.

Sutherland, Zena, selector. *The Orchard Book of Nursery Rhymes.* Illus. by Faith Jacques. Orchard, 1990. A book for sharing, this collection contains familiar nursery rhymes as well as popular tongue twisters and nonsense rhymes.

Yolen, Jane, editor. *Jane Yolen's Mother Goose Songbook.* Illus. by Rosekrans Hoffman. Boyds Mills, 1992. A medley of familiar nursery rhymes for parents and children to sing together. Musical arrangements are included for each selection.

Aardema, Verna, reteller. *Traveling to Tondo: A Tale of the Nkundo of Zaire.* Illus. by Will Hillenbrand. Knopf, 1991. Bowane the cat is on his way to his bride's village with wedding gifts for her. Foolishly, he allows many delays to stall his arrival. When he finally arrives he finds she is long married.

Allen, Linda. *The Mouse Bride: A Tale from Finland.* Illus. by author. Putnam, 1992. Three brothers search for brides according to the instruction of a wise old Lapp woman. Jukka, the youngest, marries a mouse who, true to folktale form, is really a bewitched princess.

Craig, Helen. *The Town Mouse and the Country Mouse.* Illus. by author. Candlewick, 1992. A new edition of a familiar tale. Here the town mouse ends the story by going off to the theatre in white tie and tails. The cartoon-like illustrations match the high jinx of the story.

de la Mare, Walter. *The Turnip.* Illus. by Kevin Hawkes. Godine, 1992. A friendly, generous peasant is kind to a stranger. When he is rewarded for his goodness, his greedy brother pretends to kindliness, too, but is soon exposed for the mean-spirited character he really is.

de Paola, Tomie. *Strega Nona.* Illus. by author. Prentice-Hall, 1975. Strega Nona could do magic, she could cure headaches and other problems. Big Anthony tries to discover the secrets of Strega Nona's magic and has to eat the consequences of his own foolishness.

Francesca, Martin, adapter. *The Honey Hunters.* Illus. by adapter. Candlewick, 1992. An African folktale explaining why animals no longer live in harmony. After they reach the honey tree they all quarrel about sharing until elephant proclaims they can never be friends again.

Gerson, Mary-Joan. *Why the Sky Is Far Away.* Illus. by Carla Golembe. Little, Brown, 1992. A Nigerian tale about a time when the sky was so close to earth people could break off pieces and eat it. But they grew greedy and wasted good food, so the sky moved far away and since then people have to plow and hunt for their food.

Grimm, The Brothers. *The Traveling Musicians of Bremen.* retold by P.K. Page. Illus. by Kady MacDonald Denton. Little, Brown, 1992. Whimsical illustrations and conversational language lend a modern touch to the story. The robbers are outlandishly dressed teenagers and their leader is a girl, but still the musicians work their wondrous trick.

Kellogg, Steven. *Mike Fink.* Illus. by author. Morrow, 1992. Mike Fink, King of the Keelboatmen, outwrestles grizzly bears and single-handedly defeats all the other boatmen in this traditional American tall tale.

Kimmel, Eric A. *The Tale of Aladdin and the Wonderful Lamp*. Illus. by Ju-Hong Chen. Holiday, 1992. A sly tale showing Aladdin as a lazy fellow who relies on his magic lamp and genie to win the sultan's daughter and all the riches he wants until he's tricked out of the lamp.

Kimmel, Eric A. *Anansi Goes Fishing*. Illus. by Janet Stevens. Holiday, 1992. Why do spiders spin webs? It's because of the time Anansi tried to trick Turtle into catching a fish and cooking it for him. But this time lazy Anansi weaves the nets and catches the fish while Turtle gets to eat the fish.

Louie, Ai-Ling. *Yeh-Shen: A Cinderella Story from China*. Illus. by Ed Young. Philomel, 1982. A fish plays the role of the fairy godmother and the magic slipper still reunites the lovers in this version of Cinderella.

Perrault, Charles. *Puss in Boots*. Illus. by Fred Marcellino. FS&G, 1990. From the flourish of his feathered hat to his knee-high leather boots, Puss is ever the gallant hero in this tale of friendship and fidelity.

Rounds, Glen, reteller. *Three Little Pigs and the Big Bad Wolf*. Illus. by reteller. Holiday, 1992. The wolf is all bad-guy, eating the first two pigs and huffing and puffing as hard as he can, until he gets his comeuppance at the hands of the third pig in this traditional retelling of a favorite story.

Winthrop, Elizabeth, adapter. *Vasilissa the Beautiful: A Russian Folktale.* Illus. by Alexander Koshkin. HarperCollins, 1991. Vasilissa's evil stepmother sends her into the dark forest alone. She meets Baba Yaga, the witch with chicken feet, and takes a glowing skull from her to defeat her enemies.

Dance

Brighton, Catherine. *Nijinsky: Scenes from the Childhood of the Great Dancer.* Doubleday, 1989. Scenes from the great ballet star's childhood in Russia show him auditioning at the Imperial Ballet School where he became a star at a young age. The excitement of opening nights and premiers is very real.

Gauch, Patricia Lee. *Bravo, Tanya.* Illus. by Satomi Ichikawa. Philomel, 1990. Tanya is excited about going to her first ballet lesson. Trouble develops when she misses a pirouette and falls. When she dances at home with her bear, perfection is achieved.

Hoffman, Mary. *Amazing Grace.* Illus. by Caroline Binch. Dial, 1991. Grace is sad when classmates tell her she can't play Peter Pan because she's a girl and black. After seeing an African-American ballerina perform Grace knows she can be anything she wants to be.

Isadora, Rachel. *Opening Night.* Illus. by author. Greenwillow, 1984. Young readers share in the excitement — and nervousness — of opening night with Heather as she prepares for her ballet debut.

Kuklin, Susan. *Going to My Ballet Class.* Bradbury, 1989. Follow Jami to her first ballet lessons! Share her excitement as she displays the dedication and discipline the class develops working together their first year. Photos of Jami and her classmates capture the experience.

Littledale, Freya. *The Twelve Dancing Princesses: A Folktale from the Brothers Grimm.* Illus. by Isadore Seltzer. Scholastic, 1988. Every night twelve princesses secretly go dancing. They dance merrily until they have worn holes in their shoes, returning home tired but happy as dawn breaks.

McCully, Emily Arnold. *Mirette on the High Wire.* Illus. by author. Putnam, 1992. It is Paris in the last century where Mirette is a student of Bellini, the famous high-wire walker. She practices with the concentration of a ballet dancer until she performs with him high above the streets of Paris.

McKissack, Patricia C. *Mirandy and Brother Wind.* Illus. by Jerry Pinkney. Knopf, 1988. Mirandy schemes to get Brother Wind to help her win the Junior Cakewalk dance contest in the rural South during the 1920s.

Martin, Bill, Jr. *Barn Dance.* Illus. by Ted Rand. Holt, 1986. A boy creeps out to the barn at night to watch a barn dance. He is delighted by the music, the dancing, and the happy feelings he sees. The rhythm of a barn dance is conveyed through the rhythm of the story's verse.

Mathers, Petra. *Sophie and Lou.* HarperCollins, 1991. Shy Sophie watches the fun other mice are having at the dance studio and borrows a library book about learning to dance. One night as she dances along to the Studio's music her bell rings, bashful Lou has come to ask Sophie for a dance.

Richardson, Jean. *Clara's Dancing Feet.* Illus. by Joanna Carey. Putnam, 1987. Clara loves to dance and is excited about going to dance class. When she gets there she is overcome by nerves and shyness until she gains some confidence.

Stapler, Sarah. *Cordelia, Dance!* Illus. by author. Dial, 1990. Cordelia the crocodile really wants to learn to dance. Instead, her clumsiness causes havoc in dance class until she meets an even clumsier dancer.

Aliki. *Milk: From Cow to Carton.* Illus. by author. HarperCollins, 1992. How does a carton of milk get to the breakfast table? Follow along as milk moves through the dairy process until it is bottled and ready to go to the supermarket.

Balestrino, Philip. *The Skeleton Inside You.* Illus. by True Kelley. Crowell, 1989. A simple text and cartoonlike illustrations explain how the human skeleton fits together and functions, how to keep it healthy, and what happens when a bone breaks.

Cobb, Vicki. *Feeding Yourself.* Illus. by Marylin Hafner. Lippincott, 1989. No one knows who invented silverware or chopsticks but they have been used for hundreds of years. Read how people who first ate with forks were considered strange and how silverware has changed over time.

Gibbons, Gail. *Catch the Wind.* Illus. by author. Little, Brown, 1989. Katie and Sam visit Ike's kite shop where they learn how different types of kites are made and what makes them fly. Simple instructions for constructing a kite and bold, bright graphics in primary colors enchance the text.

Fritz, Jean. *The Great Adventure of Christopher Columbus.* Illus. by Tomie de Paola. Putnam,

1992. A pop-up book that lets young children follow right along on the voyage with Columbus and his crew. The full-color illustrations capture the crew's sense of wonder and discovery as they sail an uncharted course.

Griffin, Sandra Ure. *Earth Circles.* Illus. by author. Walker, 1989. A mother and daughter climb a hill on an early spring day to celebrate the cycle of a year. The text on each facing page is set in a circle and gives an explanation of nature's life cycle of rebirth and nurturing.

Jones, Brian. *Space: A Three-Dimensional Journey.* Illus. by Richard Clifton-Dey. Dial, 1991. Spectacular! Volcanoes erupt violently on Io, Jupiter's moon and dust storms swirl across Mars in a realistic tour of the planets. Brief text accompanies the pop-up art.

Llewellyn, Claire. *My First Book of Time.* Photos. Dorling Kindersley, 1992. Calendars, seasons, and different types of timepieces are discussed in easy to understand terms. There are simple experiments for measuring time and a foldout clock with a puzzle makes the subject real.

Maass, Robert. *When Autumn Comes.* Photos by author. Holt, 1990. Words and bright photographs depict what happens in autumn as leaves turn color, birds fly south, and children return to school. People are shown preparing for the coming of winter.

Maestro, Betsy. *Snow Day.* Illus. by Giulio Maestro. Scholastic, 1989. Where does the snow go, how are airports and highways cleared of snow so people and products can move again? All of this is shown as a family spends a snow day at home waiting for the city to start again.

Ormerod, Jan. *When We Went to the Zoo.* Illus. by author. Lothrop, 1991. Share the excitement as a brother and sister visit the zoo with their father. They pet a boa constrictor, go for a camel ride, and watch the sea lions being fed.

Selsam, Millicent, and Joyce Hunt. *Keep Looking!* Illus. by Normand Chartier. Macmillan, 1989. A snow-covered house in the country appears deserted but on each page a small animal has setted in for the winter. Readers are asked how many animals they can find, answers are given on the last page.

Animals All Around

Arnosky, Jim. *Otters Under Water.* Illus. by author. Putnam, 1992. Two young otters swim and play in a pond abounding with plants and other wildlife while their mother watches. The simple text, one short sentence on a page, is just right for beginning readers.

Bernhard, Emery. *Ladybug.* Illus. by Durga Bernhard. Holiday, 1992. A ladybug marches across the pages drawing the text together into a seamless combination of science, history, and folklore of ladybugs.

Blumberg, Rhoda. *Jumbo.* Illus. by Jonathan Hunt. Bradbury, 1992. The biggest star of P.T. Barnum's circus, the elephant whose name gave meaning to the word *jumbo*, started life as a scrawny creature. His life and tragic death are a memorable reading adventure.

Gibbons, Gail. *Say Woof! The Day of a Country Veterinarian.* Macmillan, 1992. Spend a day with a vet while he examines pets brought to his office, then go into the operating room with him. Share the doctor's enthusiasm for his work when he visits farms, caring for sick or hurt animals later in the day.

Guiberson, Brenda Z. *Spoonbill Swamp.* Illus. by Megan Lloyd. Holt, 1992. Young naturalists will enjoy spending a day in a swamp with an alligator and a spoonbill bird family, avoiding their enemies and foraging for food. The story also contains ecological information about the swamp ecosystem.

McDonald, Megan. *Is This a House for Hermit Crab?* Illus. by S.D. Schindler. Orchard, 1990. Hermit Crab has outgrown his house and must find a bigger one before the pricklepine fish finds him. Everything he tries is too big, too deep, too full of holes, until he finds an empty snail shell.

Machotka, Hana. *Breathtaking Noses.* Photos by author. Morrow, 1992. Readers may not think noses are special until they try to guess which animal the nose belongs to and what is special about it. An intriguing look at how animals adapt to their environment in a guessing game format.

McNulty, Faith. *Orphan: The Story of a Baby Woodchuck.* Illus. by Darby Morrell. Scholastic, 1992. The author takes an orphaned woodchuck into her home to raise and soon realizes she must teach Chuck to live on his own in the woods regardless of how much she cares about him.

Parnall, Peter. *Stuffer.* Illus. by author. Macmillan, 1992. A special story for horse lovers. The love of a young girl for her high-jumping colt is lovingly told. Then the horse is sold. He is finally given to another loving youngster in a dramatic finale.

Pedersen, Judy. *The Tiny Patient.* Illus. by author. Knopf, 1989. A child and her grandmother find a sparrow with a broken wing. With their tender, loving care the bird's wing heals until it is ready to fly away again.

Richardson, Judith Benet. *The Way Home.* Illus. by Salley Mavor. Macmillan, 1991. Savi, a baby elephant, enjoys a day at the beach with her mother and doesn't want to return to the jungle. Finally, linked trunk to tail, Savi and her mother find their way home by the light of a bright, banana-shaped moon.

Roop, Peter and Connie Roop. *One Earth, A Multitude of Creatures.* Illus. by Valerie Kells. Walker, 1992. Featuring animals of the Northwest, each double-page spread shows an animal engaged in its daily routine of survival.

Schoenherr, John. *Bear.* Illus. by author. Philomel, 1991. Bear is no longer a cub and must look after himself in the vast northern wilderness. He is still scared by noises and shadows until he rises and lets out a deep growl, ready to protect himself and his rightful place in nature.

Sill, Cathryn. *About Birds: A Guide for Children.* Illus. by John Sill. Peachtree, 1991. Simple short sentences and detailed watercolor illustrations introduce beginning readers to several species of familiar birds nestled in their regular settings.

Tejima. *Owl Lake.* Illus. by author. Philomel, 1987. Breathtaking double-page woodcuts show an owl family in night flight at a lake. Father owl catches a fish in his claws and brings it back for his family to share in this simple nature story.

Chapter 9

Seven and Eight Year Olds

Sports, Hobbies, Action

Bjork, Christina. *Linnea In Monet's Garden.* Illus. by Lena Anderson. R & S Books, 1987. Linnea loves Monet's paintings; travel with her on a visit to the artist's home outside Paris.

Charlip, Remy. *Handtalk Birthday.* Four Winds, 1987. Join a joyful birthday celebration for hearing impaired Mary Beth. Children are shown how to sign simple words and numbers while the surprise party goes on.

Horvatic, Anne. *Simple Machines.* Photos by Stephen Bruner. Dutton, 1989. Everyday machines we take for granted do very complicated jobs and make our lives more fun. Levers propel seesaws and ramps serve as skateboard surfaces.

Krementz, Jill. *A Very Young Skater.* Photos by author. Knopf, 1979. The glamour and painstaking practice needed to succeed as a figure skater are lovingly portrayed in this photo essay.

Lankford, Mary. *Hopscotch Around the World.* Illus. by Karen Milone. Morrow, 1992. Play hopscotch nineteen different ways just like it is played in other countries around the world! Directions are given and each variant of the game is described with a large easy to follow illustration.

Norworth, Jack. *Take Me Out to the Ballgame.* Illus. by Alec Gillman. Four Winds, 1993. Go out with the crowd and relive the 1947 World Series between the Yankees and the Dodgers. The words and music of this familiar song recall the fierce rivalry between two home teams, the "Bronx Bombers" and "Dem Bums," in this fondly remembered World Series.

Schwartz, David M. *If You Made a Million.* Illus. by Steven Kellogg. Lothrop, 1989. With the help of Marvelosissimo the Mathematical Magician, children learn how to handle money, save it, and plan to spend it.

Smith, Robert Kimmel. *Bobby Baseball.* Illus. by Alan Tiegreen. Delacorte, 1989. Bobby dreams of being a baseball star until he plays for the team his father coaches. Filled with information and trivia about baseball, the story focuses on playing the game.

Families

Banish, Roslyn. *A Forever Family.* Photos. HarperCollins, 1992. Eight-year-old Jennifer Jordan-Wong tells the story of her adoption and how, over time, they have become a close-knit family. The story of her adoption ceremony and celebration afterward is very moving.

Bunting, Eve. *Fly Away Home.* Illus. by Ronald Himler. Clarion, 1991. A young child tells of his homeless existence living in an airport with his father, trying to escape being noticed and always hopeful they'll find a home.

Cooney, Barbara. *Miss Rumphius.* Illus. by author. Penguin, 1982. Grandfather tells young Alice she must make the world a more beautiful place when she grows up. And that is exactly what she does, planting seeds all over the countryside.

Daly, Nikki. *Not So Fast Songololo.* Illus. by author. Puffin, 1986. On a shopping trip to the village marketplace in South Africa, Grandmother and Malusi tolerate each other's pace.

Garza, Carmen Lomas. *Family Pictures/Cuadros de Familia.* Illus. by author. Children's Book Press, 1990. Using both English and Spanish text, the author writes about her childhood. She tells about being part of a loving extended family and celebrating holidays in a traditional Mexican community in Texas.

Hale, Lucretia. *The Lady Who Put Salt in Her Coffee.* Adapted and Illus. by Amy Schwartz. HB, 1989. Mrs. Peterkin puts salt in her coffee instead of sugar and the family spends the day trying to fix it. In their silliness they consult lots of people until someone suggests making another pot. Adapted from *The Peterkin Papers.*

Heide, Florence Parry, and Judith Heide Gilliland. *The Day of Ahmed's Secret.* Illus. by Ted Lewin. Lothrop, 1990. As he steers his donkey cart through the streets of Cairo, Ahmed is bursting with a great secret he can't wait to share with his family. Later he proudly writes his name in Arabic, sharing his secret with his family at last.

Isadora, Rachel. *At the Crossroads.* Illus. by author. Greenwillow, 1991. Young children eagerly await their fathers' return to their village after a long absence working in the mines. The illustrations reflect the story's South African setting, while the emotions of love and anticipation are universal.

MacLachlan, Patricia. *Sarah, Plain and Tall.* HarperCollins, 1985. When Papa advertises for a new wife, Anna and Caleb try to recall memories of their mother even as their love embraces Sarah.

MacLachlan, Patricia. *Three Names.* Illus. by Alexander Pertzoff. HarperCollins, 1991. A child and his great-grandfather take turns recalling the old man's dog, Three Names, who liked to go to school with him. They tell how the dog would bark at the sun and clouds and dance around the wagon going to school.

Mosel, Arlene. *Tikki Tikki Tembo.* Illus. by Blair Lent. Holt, 1968. Back in the days when first-born sons were honored with long names, Chang's brother falls down a well. The results are nearly disastrous when Chang has to quicky repeat his name so his brother can be rescued.

Parish, Peggy. *Amelia Bedelia.* Illus. by Fritz Siebel. HarperCollins, 1963. Poor Amelia Bedelia! She means well but she always gets it wrong. Young children howl with laughter as Amelia Bedelia dusts the furniture by putting powder on it and changes the towels by cutting new designs in them.

Smith, Maggie. *My Grandma's Chair.* Lothrop, 1992. Grandma's worn chair becomes an adventure seat for Alex as he sits in it and imagines himself on adventures to Mars in a hot-air balloon. But the best adventure of all is to sit quietly in the chair with Grandma.

Steig, William. *Brave Irene.* Illus. by author.

FS&G, 1986. The vision of her mother's face and smell of her fresh-baked bread keep Irene going through a snowstorm to deliver a gown her mother has sewn for the duchess.

Stolz, Mary. *Go Fish.* Illus. by Pat Cummings. HarperCollins, 1991. Thomas and Grandfather go trout fishing and play a quiet game of "go fish" together. Later, Grandfather tells stories about their family going back to their African roots in this beginning chapter book.

Riddles, Jokes, Puns

Base, Graeme. *The Eleventh Hour: A Curious Mystery.* Abrams, 1989. Eleven guests are invited to Horace the elephant's 11th birthday and then the food is found missing. Clues are provided, messages are hidden in illustrations and text, and the answer is contained in a sealed section at the end of the book.

Brown, Marc. *Spooky Riddles.* Illus. by author. Random House, 1984. Parents groan at the puns and children ask for more jokes just like them.

Kessler, Leonard. *Old Turtle's 90 Knock-Knocks, Jokes, and Riddles.* Illus. by author. Greenwillow, 1991. Several animals present selections of jokes that range from the merely silly to those that make parents hold their ears. Young readers delight in trying these out on each other.

Levine, Caroline. *Riddles to Tell Your Cat.* Illus. by Meyer Seltzer. Whitman, 1992. Kids who love cats will love these riddles! Divided into short chapters, each one deals with a theme familiar to children and their cats.

Mathews, Judith, and Fay Robinson. *Oh, How Waffle! Riddles You Can Eat.* Illus. by Carl Whiting. Whitman, 1993. Puns and wordplay abound but the emphasis is on the silliness. There are riddles about bagels and microwave ovens, all illustrated with scenes of madcap mayhem.

O'Hare, Jeffrey, editor. *Knee Slappers, Side Splitters, and Tummy Ticklers; A Book of Riddles and Jokes.* Boyds Mills, 1992. Just plain, good, old-fashioned plays on words to tickle young readers' funny bones.

Patz, Nancy. *Moses Supposes His Toeses Are Roses.* Illus. by author. HB, 1984. Contains every known tongue twister and many funny ones never heard before; good for hours of silly practice on a rainy afternoon.

Rees, Ennis. *Fast Freddie Frog and Other Tongue-Twister Rhymes.* Illus. by John O'Brien. Boyds Mills, 1992. From the sublime to the ridiculous, these tongue twisters are nearly impossible to repeat because children have a hard time talking and laughing at the same time. The illustrations extend the verbal jokes.

Smith, Barry. *Cumberland Road.* Illus. by author. Houghton, 1989. One title in the Can You Find? series asks readers to find household items that have become lost. The illustrations are very solidly packed and it takes good detective work to locate all the missing items.

Schwartz, Alvin. *Busy Buzzing Bumblebees and Other Tongue Twisters,* 2d ed. Illus. by Paul Meisel. HarperCollins, 1992. Leave this one to the kids, it delights their sense of humor to practice saying tongue twisters. Some are new, some are tried and true, all are perfect for beginning readers.

Terban, Marvin. *Eight Ate: A Feast of Homonym Riddles.* Illus. by Giulio Maestro. Clarion, 1982. Eight ate when four couples went to a restaurant. The answers to all the riddles involve words that sound alike but are spelled differently, providing lots of opportunities for silly word combinations and read-aloud fun.

Wiesner, David. *Tuesday.* Illus. by author. Clarion, 1991. The humor is real in a surreal world where frogs on lily pads fly over a sleeping village. Sunrise breaks the spell until next Tuesday when pigs take to the air.

Bemelmans, Ludwig. *Madeline.* Illus. by author. Viking, 1939. A classic story set in Paris of Madeline and her schoolmates, "twelve little girls in two straight lines." Madeline, a derring-do heroine, is a constant challenge to Miss Clavel. There are five other Madeline titles in this series.

Blume, Judy. *Freckle Juice.* Illus. by Sonia Lisker. Scholastic, 1971. More than anything in the world Andrew longed to have freckles like his friend, Nicky. A perfect and perfectly funny short novel for young readers.

Byars, Betsy. *Hooray for the Golly Sisters!* Illus. by Sue Truesdell. HarperCollins, 1990. In this humorous I Can Read book sisters May-May and Rose travel west in their covered wagon. Along the way they stop to entertain enthusiastic audiences in the towns they pass through, always having a good time themselves.

Cameron, Ann. *Julian's Glorious Summer.* Illus. by Dora Leder. Random House, 1987. Julian starts some major trouble when he can't admit to his friend Gloria that he is afraid to ride a bike. There are other titles about Julian; look for *The Stories Julian Tells* and *More Stories Julian Tells.*

Clifton, Lucille. *Three Wishes.* Illus. by Michael Hays. Doubleday, 1992. When Zenobia finds a lucky penny with her birth year on it, she wishes for her best friend, Victorius, to show up. Her wish comes true and the two friends spend New Year's Day together.

de Regniers, Beatrice Schenk. *A Week in the Life of Best Friends, and Other Poems of Friendship.* Illus. by Nancy Doyle. Scholastic, 1988. The joys, frustrations, and fun of sharing experiences with a best friend are celebrated in nine humorous poems.

Dugan, Barbara. *Loop the Loop.* Illus. by James Stevenson. Greenwillow, 1992. Their friendship develops when elderly Mrs. Simpson shows Anne her tricks with a yo-yo. When Mrs. Simpson must enter a nursing home, Anne trades her doll, Eleanor, for Bertrand, Mrs. Simpson's cat who is not allowed in the home.

Koller, Jackie French. *Fish Fry Tonight.* Illus. by Catharine O'Neill. Crown, 1992. The fish that Mama Mouse catches gets bigger and bigger with each retelling as her friends join her to share in eating it. Clever Mama feeds all her friends by sending out for a hundred pizzas.

McLerran, Alice. *Roxaboxen.* Illus. by Barbara Cooney. Lothrop, 1991. Join a group of best friends in their imaginary town where Marian is the mayor and everyone gets to make the rules.

Mills, Lauren. *The Rag Coat.* Illus. by author. Little, Brown, 1991. Her classmates laugh at her when Minna comes to school in a quilted coat sewn from scraps until she explains that her coat is full of their stories, that the scraps have all come from their homes.

Polacco, Patricia. *Chicken Sunday.* Illus. by author. Philomel, 1992. The author recalls her friendship with two African-American brothers and their grandmother, Miss Eula. There is trouble when they try to buy her an Easter bonnet, but their friendship saves the day and Miss Eula gets her bonnet.

Viorst, Judith. *I'll Fix Anthony.* Illus. by Arnold Lobel. HarperCollins, 1969. Anthony's younger brother plots and plans all the ways he's going to get even with Anthony, but not until he gets bigger.

Yorinks, Arthur. *Hey, Al.* Illus. by Richard Egielski. FS&G, 1986. Al, a janitor, and his best friend, Eddie, a small terrier, long for a new life of ease and comfort. What they get isn't exactly what they wished for.

Series Books

Bond, Michael. *A Bear Called Paddington.* Illus. by Peggy Fortnum. Houghton, 1958. Straight from darkest Peru comes the series about the lovable but bumbling bear, Paddington. He lives in London with the Brown family and can't seem to resist courting disaster at every turn. Many titles are available.

Calhoun, Mary. *High-Wire Henry.* Illus. by Erick Ingraham. Morrow, 1991. Henry, the Siamese cat, rescues the new puppy and ensures his position in the family when he becomes a high-wire walker on the telephone line. Other books in the series are *Hot-Air Henry* and *Cross-Country Cat.*

Cleary, Beverly. *Ramona and Her Father.* Illus. Morrow, 1975. Ramona tries all kinds of schemes to cheer her family when her father loses his job.

Giff, Patricia Reilly. *Sunny-Side Up.* Illus. by Blanche Sims. Dell, 1986. Beast and his best friend, Matthew, have their last exciting adventures before Matthew moves away. Any title in the Kids of the Polk Street School series will delight beginning chapter book readers and make them laugh.

Hughes, Shirley. *Wheels.* Illus. by author. Lothrop, 1991. All the children on Trotter Street have toys with wheels and Carlos wants a shiny new bicycle just like Billy's. His brother builds him the best red birthday surprise of all. This is a new story in the Tale of Trotter Street series.

Lindgren, Astrid. *Pippi Longstocking.* Illus. by

Louis Glanzman. Viking, 1957. An indomitable character, Pippi lives alone with her horse and monkey, Mr. Nilsson. Her outrageous behavior appeals to children's imaginations.

Nabb, Magdalen. *Josie Smith*. Illus. by Pirkko Vainio. Macmillan, 1988. Josie Smith learns the difference between being naughty and making a mistake when she tries taking charge of things in a popular new series of short chapter stories.

Rylant, Cynthia. *Henry and Mudge and the Bedtime Thumps*. Bradbury, 1991. Henry worries whether his grandmother will like his beloved dog, Mudge. Will Mudge drool on Grandma, will Mudge have to sleep outside, all alone, on a trip to Grandma's house. A delightful series for beginning readers.

Sharmat, Marjorie Weinman. *Nate the Great Stalks Stupidweed*. Illus. by Marc Simont. Coward-McCann, 1986. One title in a very popular, easy-to-read mystery series. Nate and his dog, Sludge, comb the neighborhood looking for clues, keeping young readers trying to guess the solution.

Folktales

Cooper, Susan. *The Selkie Girl*. Illus. by Warwick Hutton. Aladdin, 1986. A retelling of the

Scottish legend of the fisherman who takes a seal woman, a selkie, for his bride and how she longs to return to the sea. The love of her children frees her to return to the sea.

Ehlert, Lois. *Moon Rope: A Peruvian Folktale.* Illus. by author. HB, 1992. Published with both English and Spanish texts on a page. Fox fashions a grass rope to climb to the moon and persuades reluctant Mole to accompany him. Mole slips down into the earth, where he lives still. Fox's face can be seen on nights when the moon is full.

Goble, Paul. *Crow Chief.* Illus. by author. Orchard, 1992. From the Plains Indians comes the story of why crows are always black feathered and how Falling Star saves the Indian nation from starvation.

Kherdian, David, reteller. *Feathers and Tails: Animal Fables from Around the World.* Illus. by Nonny Hogrogain. Philomel, 1992. There are other fables besides Aesop's, a selection from many ancient sources is offered here. Whatever their origin, they let readers see the greed and foolishness in people and animals.

Kimmel, Eric A. *Charlie Drives the Stage.* Illus. by Glen Rounds. Holiday, 1989. Not avalanches, not "bad guys," not attacking Indians, not a collapsing bridge can stop Charlie from getting Senator McCorkle to the train on time. And imagine the senator's surprise when

Charlie's real identity is revealed.

McDermott, Gerald. *Zomo the Rabbit: A Trickster Tale from West Africa.* Illus. by author. HB, 1992. Zomo the rabbit is very clever but he is not always very wise. He outwits Big Fish, Wild Cow, and Lepoard, only to become the victim of his own greediness when he asks Sky God for wisdom.

Oughton, Jerrie. *How the Stars Fell Into the Sky: A Navajo Legend.* Illus. by Lisa Desimini. Houghton, 1992. First Woman uses the stars to write the laws in the night sky. Coyote, ever the trickster, spills the stars and brings confusion and chaos to the world in this Navajo creation legend.

Parks, Van Dyke, adapter. *Jump!: The Adventures of Brer Rabbit.* Illus. by Barry Moser. HB, 1986. In this book and its companion volumes, *Jump Again!* and *Jump on Over*, Brer Rabbit performs at his wiliest. Using his wits brings its own rewards and occasional come-uppances.

Ross, Tony. *Goldilocks and the Three Bears.* Illus. by author. Viking, 1992. For youngsters who think they've outgrown folktales, this offbeat retelling of a blue-jeans wearing Goldilocks where she visits the three polar bears and watches their color television may change their minds.

Scieszka, Jon. *The True Story of the 3 Little Pigs.*

Illus. by Lane Smith. Viking, 1989. An outrageously funny retelling of this classic story from A. Wolf's point of view. It captures the sense of silliness of any true-blooded 7-and 8-year-old. *The Frog Prince Continued* is an equally offbeat retelling of the traditional story.

Steptoe, John. *Mufaro's Beautiful Daughters.* Illus. by author. Lothrop, 1987. Readers enjoy a fresh twist on the Cinderella story. This version, set in Africa, tells how two sisters, one kind and caring and one vain, compete for the king's hand in marriage.

Thurber, James. *Many Moons.* Illus. by Marc Simont. HB, 1990. New illustrations gives this beloved classic a modern look. Princess Lenore, as princesses are wont to do, asks for the moon; the Jester is the only one at court with the good sense to ask why.

Poetry

Ciardi, John. *You Read To Me, I'll Read to You.* Illus. by Edward Gorey. HarperCollins, Harper Trophy; 1962, 1987. This poetry collection comes with instructions to take your child on your lap and let him read the blue poems to you and for you to read the others. They're all nice and silly.

Cole, Joanna, selector. *A New Treasury of Children's Poetry*. Illus. by Judith Gwyn Brown. Doubleday, 1984. A joyous collection full of bright images and snappy rhythms, some are downright silly and some speak to the heart.

Esbensen, Barbara Juster. *Who Shrank My Grandmother's House? Poems of Discovery*. Illus. by Eric Beddows. HarperCollins, 1992. Twenty-three poems that invite children to exercise a sense of wonder about familiar scenes and objects.

Goldstein, Bobbye, editor. *What's On the Menu?* Illus. by Chris Demarest. Viking, 1992. A veritable feast of grotesque culinary art. Funny poems by 25 popular children's authors and cartoonlike illustrations form one extended joke about food and table manners appealing directly to this age group.

Hudson, Wade, editor. *Pass It On: African-American Poetry for Children*. Illus. by Floyd Cooper. Scholastic, 1993. Some poems express ethnic pride and emotions but all are universal in speaking to the hearts of children.

Krull, Kathleen, selector. *Gonna Sing My Head Off!* Illus. by Allen Garns. Knopf, 1992. Children know most of the sixty-two folk songs in this collection, they are all popular American songs. Each song is accompanied by a few sentences telling a little of its history and a simple musical arrangement.

Lear, Edward. *Of Pelicans and Pussycats: Poems and Limericks*. Illus. by Jill Newton. Dial, 1990. The grandest of birds with their leathery throats are having a feast trying to marry off their pelican daughter. Along with six other humorous poems and several limericks, this collection is as fresh and funny as when it was written.

Livingston, Myra Cohn, selector. *If You Ever Meet a Whale*. Illus. by Leonard Everett Fisher. Holiday, 1992. The poems and illustrations capture the mammoth size of these sea creatures. Some poems are newly written for this collection and some have been gathered from Eskimo and Indian sources.

Lobel, Arnold. *The Book of Pigericks*. Illus. by author. HarperCollins, 1983. Outrageously funny limericks featuring pigs strike at the level of second- and third-grade humor.

Merriam, Eve. *A Poem for a Pickle: Funnybone Verses*. Illus. by Sheila Hamanaka. Morrow, 1989. Twenty-eight short funny poems to make readers laugh. Each poem has its own full-color illustration full of snap and sparkle, a veritable feast for young readers.

Prelutsky, Jack, compiler. *The Random House Book of Poetry for Children*. Illus. by Arnold Lobel. Random House, 1983. A collection of tried-and-true favorites along with poems from contemporary authors arranged according to emotional themes.

Prelutsky, Jack. *Something Big Has Been Here.* Illus. by James Stevenson. Greenwillow, 1990. Something zany and funny in a short, snappy format. Sure to please youngsters when they read about the popcorn-stuffed turkey exploding or other humorous poems.

Rosen, Michael. *Itsy-Bitsy Beasties.* Illus. by Alan Baker. Carolrhoda, 1992. Thirty-one short poems about insects, spiders, worms, and other invertebrates. The selections from many countries are mostly humorous and are good choices for reading aloud.

Rossetti, Christina. *Fly Away, Fly Away Over the Sea: And Other Poems for Children.* Selected and illus. by Bernadette Watts. North-South Books. 1991. First published in 1872, these short selections celebrate nature in all its glory. To be treasured in quiet moments as well as a pleasure to read aloud.

More Dinosaurs

Aliki. *Dinosaur Bones.* Illus. by author. Crowell, 1988. A detailed, clear text explains what scientists learn about dinosaurs by studying their bones and how continuous study of dinosaur bones leads to new theories about how these prehistoric creatures lived.

Arnold, Caroline. *Dinosaur Mountain: Graveyard of the Past.* Photos by Richard Hewett. Clarion, 1989. The best mystery story is a real one. Digging up fossil remains and reconstructing dinosaur skeletons collected at Dinosaur National Monument in Utah is a mystery lover's delight.

Hopkins, Lee Bennett, compiler. *Dinosaurs.* Illus. by Murray Tinkleman. HB, 1987. Eighteen poems by favorite children's authors present different views of dinosaurs and reflections on why they became extinct.

Lauber, Patricia. *Living with Dinosaurs.* Illus. by Douglas Henderson. Bradbury, 1991. Take a trip through prehistoric swamps and forests, see all sizes of dinosaurs on land and sea just as they really lived. Finally, observe how scientists work to uncover the hidden secrets of the past.

Lauber, Patricia. *The News About Dinosaurs.* Illus. Bradbury, 1989. Conveys the excitement scientists feel when new information about dinosaurs is uncovered. Compares what scientists formerly thought with current theories based on recent archeological discoveries.

Most, Bernard. *The Littlest Dinosaurs.* Illus. by author. HB, 1989. Small dinosaurs are compared with items from a child's world: a color-adisaurus is the size of a seesaw, giving children a realistic basis for comparison. Other small dinosaurs are shown riding tricycles and going sledding.

Most, Bernard. *Where To Look for a Dinosaur.* HB, 1993. Get out a map and visit the sites where remains of twenty-five dinosaurs were found. Compare what the sites looked like in prehistoric times with what the dinosaurs would find if they returned to their habitats now.

Peters, David. *A Gallery of Dinosaurs & Other Early Reptiles.* Knopf, 1989. One hundred land and amphibious prehistoric creatures are briefly described. Four fold-out pages are included, permitting an accurate portrayal of the dinosaurs' relative sizes.

Sattler, Helen Roney. *Stegosaurs: The Solar-Powered Dinosaurs.* Illus. by Turi Mac-Combie. Lothrop, 1992. For dinosaur fans there is a map showing the locations where remains of stegosaurs have been found throughout the world. Old theories saying stegosaurs' small brain led to their extinction is effectively discarded.

Sattler, Helen Roney. *Tyrannosaurus Rex and Its Kin: the Mesozoic Monsters.* Illus. by Joyce Powzyk. Lothrop, 1989. Scientists share their newest findings about the biggest dinosaurs that ever lived. Accompanied by illustrations so real they're scary.

Exploring the World

Arnosky, Jim. *Crinkleroot's Guide to Knowing the Trees.* Illus. by author. Bradbury, 1992. On a walk through the woods, the woodsman Crinkleroot describes different types of trees, how they are used for food and shelter and more in his gentle, friendly way.

Bash, Barbara. *Desert Giant: The World of the Saguaro Cactus.* Little, Brown, 1989. A sensitive depiction of the life cycle of the giant saguaro cactus. Memorable scenes show how it sustains animal and human life on the desert.

Brusca, Maria Cristina. *On the Pampas.* Illus. by author. Holt, 1991. Spend a summer at a farm on the Argentine pampas with Brusca as she and her cousin help with a cattle roundup and learn to dance the samba at her grandmother's birthday party.

Cherry, Lynne. *A River Ran Wild.* Illus. by author. HB, 1992. A vivid presentation of the effects of pollution on a river and the towns it runs through in New England. On a hopeful note the book shows what can be done to restore the environment to its pristine state.

Hoyt-Goldsmith, Diane. *Totem Pole.* Photos by Lawrence Migdale. Holiday, 1990. David, a Tsimshian boy, proudly tells how his father carves a totem pole for the Klallam tribe in the northwest and how he helps his father. Later on they attend the ceremony for the raising of the totem pole.

Jones, Frances. *Nature's Deadly Creatures: A Pop-Up Exploration.* Dial, 1992. Be careful! Six poisonous creatures are hiding, waiting to spring out at readers as they turn the pages. A black widow spider, a scorpion, a Gila monster, and three lifelike friends rise out of the book to tell of their encounters with people.

Kahney, Regina. *Glow-in-the-Dark Book of Animal Skeletons.* Illus. by Christopher Santoro. Random House, 1992. Look at fifteen human and animal skeletons just the way they appear on x-rays, then apply a special glow-in-the-dark transparency over each one. Brief information about size and bone structure is included.

Lavies, Bianca. *Tree Trunk Traffic.* Photos by author. Dutton, 1989. A 70-year-old maple is home to various insects, birds, and animals. They live together harmoniously as the tree nurtures them.

Machotka, Hana. *Pasta Factory.* Photos by author. Houghton, 1992. Take a trip through a pasta factory in New York City with a group of children. Watch the ingredients being mixed in huge machines then packaged and readied for delivery to area stores.

Munro, Roxie. *Blimps.* Illus. by author. Dutton, 1989. Find out about how these giant airships are designed, constructed and flown. Go along on a flight over New York City with the crew of a blimp.

Peet, Bill. *Bill Peet: An Autobiography.* Houghton, 1989. In a book filled with illustrations from his beloved storybooks, Peet writes about a life spanning the major events of this century and a career at Walt Disney Studios. Perfect for reading aloud or for beginning readers with its large print and oversize format.

Rounds, Glen. *Cowboys.* Illus. by author. Holiday, 1991. Illustrations and text show what cowboys and their horses really do out on the range, taking care of cattle and rounding them up.

Ryder, Joanne. *White Bear, Ice Bear.* Illus. by Michael Rothman. Morrow, 1989. Wake up one morning and pretend you've been transported to a wintry world. As an ice bear you can dig a hole in the ice and catch a seal or sleep in the snow as the wind blows over you.

Siebert, Diane. *Sierra.* Illus. by Wendell Minor. HarperCollins, 1991. It is the Sierra Nevada mountains talking, in rhymed verse, of its origins and the plant and animal life it supports. The verse and illustrations impart a sense of the majesty of the Sierras.

Waters, Kate, and Madeline Slovenz-Low. *Lion Dancer.* Photos by Martha Cooper. Scholastic, 1990. Ernie Wan practices all year to wear the lion's head and dance in the New Year's parade in New York's Chinatown. The Lion Dance scares away evil spirits and brings the community good luck in the New Year.

Friends from Other Days

Aliki. *The King's Day.* Illus. by author. Crowell, 1989. Share a day with the king of France, Louis XIVth. Select a wig while servants dress you, later enjoy a forty course meal. Cartoon illustrations brim with details of court life.

Dalgliesh, Alice. *The Courage of Sarah Noble.* Illus. by Leonard Weisgard. Macmillan, 1954. Sarah is a real little girl living in the Connecticut wilderness in 1707 when her father has to leave. She is scared but finds the courage to stay with an Indian family, learning respect for their ways until her father's return.

Dalgliesh, Alice. *The Thanksgiving Story.* Illus. by Helen Sewell. Aladdin, 1954. Sailing aboard the *Mayflower* was a great adventure for Giles, Constance, and Damaris Hopkins. How the family survived and celebrated the First Thanksgiving was a greater adventure.

Early, Margaret, reteller. *William Tell.* Illus. by reteller. Abrams, 1991. William Tell's heroism in confronting a would-be tyrant while fighting for his country's freedom and shooting the apple off his son's head are the exciting focus of this retelling of the ancient legend.

Fradin, Dennis Brindell. *Hiawatha: Messenger of Peace.* Illus. by Jacob Arnold. Macmillan, 1992. An exciting story presents Hiawatha as a real figure, a peacemaker and founder of the Iroquois Confederacy, some of whose principles are shown to have been adopted in the U.S. Constitution.

Hall, Donald. *Ox-Cart Man.* Illus. by Barbara Cooney. Viking, 1979. Follow along with a 19th century New England farmer and his family as they tend to their farm.

Houston, Gloria. *My Great-aunt Arizona.* Illus. by Susan Condie Lamb. HarperCollins, 1992. The author's great-aunt, born in a log cabin in Appalachia in the 1870s, dreamed of a bigger world. Arizona's story shines with joy as she teaches fourth grade in Henson Creek, often bringing her baby to class.

Levinson, Nancy Smiler. *Snowshoe Thompson.* Illus. by Joan Sandin. HarperCollins, 1992. An I Can Read adventure story about a winter trek across the Sierra Nevadas on skis a century ago. The skis have to be handmade and most people think Thompson is reckless, but a small boy has faith he will make it.

Lindbergh, Reeve. *Johnny Appleseed.* Illus. by Kathy Jakobsen. Little, Brown, 1990. Travel across the United States a century ago with Johnny Appleseed, planting apple trees that still bear fruit today. The rhymed text and paintings evoke the spirit of the American frontier.

Marzollo, Jean. *Happy Birthday, Martin Luther King.* Illus. by Brian Pinkney. Scholastic, 1993. The emphasis is on the special qualities of Martin Luther King's personality, on what makes him so universally appealing and memorable for all Americans.

Rylant, Cynthia. *When I Was Young in the Mountains.* Illus. by Diane Goode. Dutton, 1982. The author remembers what it was like growing up in the mountains, surrounded by a close-knit, loving family. There was no indoor plumbing, electricity, or television but there was a strong sense of community and love.

Waters, Kate. *Sarah Morton's Day.* Photos by Russ Kendall. Scholastic, 1989. Sarah's day begins at sun-up in Plymouth colony with tending the fire and feeding the chickens. There is time for playing with friend Elizabeth and for a brief reading lesson during her busy day.

Chapter 10

Nine and Ten Year Olds

Series Books

Cooper, Ilene. *The Kids From Kennedy Middle School*. Morrow, 1992. Several titles are available in this series featuring a lively cast of characters and well-structured story lines. *The New, Improved Gretchen Hubbard* (1992) is the latest entry available.

Howe, James. *Bunnicula, A Rabbit's Tale of Mystery*. Atheneum, 1992. There are now five titles in this sought after series about, possibly, a vampire bunny. The stories offer a satisfying blend of fantasy, mystery, and humor.

Jacques, Brian. *Mattimeo*. Philomel, 1990. Another tale in the series about Redwall Abbey. This time Slagar the Cruel plots to seek his revenge against Matthias, the mouse warrior and gets the whole kingdom up in arms against him.

Lowry, Lois. *Anastasia Has the Answers*. Houghton, 1986. Another in the series of light-hearted, breezy stories about Anastasia Krupnik. Her cares and worries about friendship, love, and growing up get written into her journal and tried out on her friends. *Attaboy, Sam!* is the newest title in this popular series.

Martin, Ann M. *The Baby-sitters Club series*. Scholastic, 1986. Any title in this wildly popular series is sure to please young readers as they follow the adventures of seven friends and the baby-sitting business they run.

Naylor, Phyllis Reynolds. *All but Alice*. Atheneum, 1992. Alice is a seventh-grader who wants to say the right things, wear the right clothes, and be part of the in crowd at school. It all starts to come together for her in this title until she has to make choices.

Norton, Mary. *The Borrowers*. Illus. by Beth and Joe Krush. HB, 1952, 1980. About the size of a hat-pin, the Borrowers live in out of the way places in people's homes and exist by borrowing from humans. Arrietty is discovered by a visiting boy and eventually they have to emigrate.

Peck, Robert Newton. *Soup in Love*. Illus. by Charles Robinson. Delacorte, 1992. Soup and his friend Rob hatch a scheme to win first place in a Valentine's Day contest with all kinds of disastrous mishaps along the way.

This is one of many humorous titles in a very popular series.

Sobol, Donald J. *Encyclopedia Brown and the Case of the Disgusting Sneakers*. Morrow, 1990. Encyclopedia Brown, boy detective, invites readers to match wits with him as he goes about solving mysteries. Ten solve-it-yourself mysteries replete with clues and solutions provide a challenge to readers.

Wilder, Laura Ingalls. *Little House series*. Illus. by Garth Williams. HarperCollins, 1953. There are nine books in this series recounting frontier life, its hardships and its joys, in the late 1800s for Laura and her family.

Horses

Farley, Walter. *The Black Stallion*. Random House, 1989. After helping the Black stallion survive a shipwreck, Alex's dream of taming the wild Arabian horse and entering him in a race comes true. There are many books about the black stallion and his offspring in this popular series.

Henry, Marguerite. *Misty of Chincoteague*. Illus. by Wesley Dennis. Macmillan, 1947. At the annual running of the wild ponies on Chincoteague Island, the wildest mare of all is purchased by two young children who are surprised at the birth of the Arabian colt, Misty. The story continues in an ever-popular series.

Jurmain, Suzanne. *Once Upon a Horse*. Lothrop, 1989. Horses have served people loyally. This book tells how horses have helped shape human history, served in war, at work, and at play through the ages and in all places.

Martin, Katherine. *Night Riding*. Knopf, 1989. More than anything else, Prin loves riding horses. When she goes riding alone at night she makes a disturbing discovery.

Patent, Dorothy Hinshaw. *Where the Wild Horses Roam*. Photos by William Munoz. Clarion, 1989. Horse round-ups in the old wild west were glamorous, but can the wild stallion population survive now? Ride along to a wild mustang refuge and read how the wild horse population is managed.

Peyton, K. M. *Poor Badger*. Illus. by Mary Lonsdale. Delacorte, 1992. Ros and her friend, Leo, rescue a horse they observe being neglected and abused. Her efforts to find a home for Badger when she realizes she can't keep him are valiant.

Saville, Lynn. *Horses in the Circus Ring*. Photos by author. Dutton, 1989. Circuses are always exciting and reading about how circus horses are trained to perform their tricks and stunts leaves readers holding their breath. Photos from several circuses capture the thrill of performing.

Sherlock, Patti. *Four of a Kind*. Holiday, 1991. Andy borrows money to buy a pair of percherons, work horses. His goal is to win the horse-pulling contest at the state fair and he works hard to reach his goal, not letting any obstacle or hardship deter him along the way.

Slade, Michael. *The Horses of Central Park*. Scholastic, 1992. Wendell develops the ability to communicate with the horses he visits every day. When he learns of their unsympathetic treatment by their carriage drivers he and his best friend, Judith, hatch a plot to rescue them.

Mysteries, Fantasy

Banks, Lynne Reid. *The Indian In the Cupboard*. Doubleday, 1980. Omri receives a plastic Indian for his birthday and discovers the Indian can come alive. Together they travel back in time to the Old West for exciting adventures.

Bellairs, John. *The Spell of the Sorcerer's Skull*. Dial, 1984. Combining mystery and supernatural events, another adventure of the boy detective, Johnny Dixon, will set reader's teeth on edge. There are demons, howling and unearthly noises, and a haunted dollhouse to activate eager imaginations.

Cohen, Daniel. *Great Ghosts*. Illus. by David Linn. Dutton, 1990. Nine ghost stories to set readers' spines tingling and their teeth chattering. Read at your own risk only when someone trustworthy is nearby.

Eager, Edward. *Half Magic*. Illus. by N. M. Bodecker. HB, 1954, 1982. When the children find a lucky charm that grants half a wish they are ready to go on great adventures. They overcome the problem and are transported through time.

Kehret, Peg. *Horror At the Haunted House*. Dutton, 1992. Ellen realizes she is being haunted by a ghost who's been dead for three years. While preparing a Halloween haunted house, Ellen confronts the ghost and solves the mystery.

Mahy, Margaret. *Dangerous Spaces*. Viking, 1991. Anthea is glad at first to escape her uncle's noisy home and enter the quiet space of Viridian, but slowly Viridian takes over her whole life and controls her mind. A spellbinding fantasy from a master storyteller.

Park, Ruth. *My Sister Sif*. Viking, 1991. In the undersea world where Riko and Sif live in the near future, merpeople are able to communicate with sea creatures. Pollution is the threat they face in this ecological fantasy.

Sherman, Josepha. *Child of Faerie, Child of Earth*. Walker, 1992. Percinet, the handsome faerie prince is in love with Graciosa, a young girl unaware of her own faerie heritage. How she overcomes the bonds of her evil stepmother to accept her magical fate inspires this romantic fantasy.

Stevenson, Drew. *Toying with Danger*. Illus. by Marcy Ramsey. Dutton, 1993. Sarah hears there's a Frankenstein monster at her grandfather's farm. He's a toy inventor so that mystery is easily solved, then Sarah and her friends get busy solving the mystery of who's trying to steal his new inventions.

Turner, Ann. *Rosemary's Witch*. HarperCollins, 1991. A plague of toads, a freezing fog in July — the community is rattled by such extraordinary events. Only nine-year-old Rosemary has the courage to confront a 150-year-old witch.

Friends

Brooks, Bruce. *Everywhere*. HarperCollins, 1990. Will soul switching work? After his grandfather's heart attack, a young boy and his new friend, Dooley, join forces in a magic ritual they hope will save grandfather's life.

Cleary, Beverly. *Dear Mr. Henshaw.* Illus. by Paul O. Zelinsky. Morrow, 1983. Leigh Botts doesn't have many friends and he misses his dad since he left. Through his letters to Mr. Henshaw, his favorite author, Leigh is encouraged to write a prizewinning story.

Danziger, Paula. *The Cat Ate My Gymsuit.* Delacorte, 1974. Marcy is upset at being overweight and not having friends. She blossoms, gaining in self-confidence, when she comes to the aid of her favorite teacher.

Getz, David. *Thin Air.* Holt, 1990. Jacob suffers from asthma. When he gets to his new school the teacher has told the class about him. And then there's his big brother to put up with until Jacob finds a solution to his asthma and a friend in his brother.

Hamilton, Virginia. *Cousins.* Philomel, 1990. Cousins can be best friends, too. But sometimes they can be really jealous and fight all the time. When Cammy and Patty Ann fight, Cammy is left with no way to say "I'm sorry."

Paterson, Katherine. *The Great Gilly Hopkins.* Crowell, 1978. Gilly has been in foster care for most of her life and is determined to upset Mrs. Trotter with her usual tricks. A surprise visitor helps her learn that what you wish for isn't always what you really want.

Pevsner, Stella. *The Night the Whole Class Slept*

Over. Clarion, 1991. Dan can't resign himself to moving to the isolated north woods with his mother, he resists even thinking about it and concentrates instead on being the new kid in class and making new friends.

Porte, Barbara Ann. *Fat Fanny, Beanpole Bertha, and the Boys*. Illus. by Maxie Chambliss. Orchard, 1991. When faced with family problems Fanny resorts to eating, her friend Bertha is unable to eat. What keeps both girls going is the friendship they share, the secrets they can confide in each other.

Smith, Robert Kimmel. *Jelly Belly*. Illus. by Bob Jones. Dell, 1981. Ned doesn't really want to be fat, he'd love to lose weight. Even a summer at a diet camp doesn't help him until he discovers the secret for himself.

Woodson, Jacqueline. *Last Summer with Maizon*. Delacorte, 1990. Best friends forever, that's what Maizon and Margaret promise each other until Maizon is chosen to attend an exclusive boarding school and, they both fear, be the only African-American student there.

Poetry

Axelrod, Alan, compiler. *Songs of the Wild West*. Illus. Simon & Schuster, 1991. Musical arrangements and art from several museums accompany this collection of classic ballads and hearty work songs. Historical commentary about the songs is included.

Booth, David, selector. 'Til All the Stars Have Fallen. Illus. by Kady MacDonald Denton. Viking, 1990. Subjects of interest to children such as dinosaurs, nature, playing, and the seasons form the core of this collection. Poems about Native Americans, various ethnic groups, and both genders are reflected in the illustrations.

Harrison, David L. Somebody Catch My Homework. Illus. by Betsy Lewin. Wordsong, 1992. Tim has good manners, he won't spit out his gum until the President comes to school and says "please." The kids in this school know all about cafeteria food (UGH), doing homework (AGONY), and reading (JOY).

Joseph, Lynn A. Coconut Kind of Day. Illus. by Sandra Speidel. Puffin Books, 1992. The flavor of the Caribbean abounds in poems that tell of buying ices from the "palet man" and drinking sweet coconut water. Other poems about steel drum bands and cricket games re-create the rhythm of island life.

Lewis, Claudia. Up In the Mountains: And Other Poems of Long Ago. Illus. by Joel Fontaine. HarperCollins, 1991. A sense of family life in a small town early in the century is created in these sixteen poems. The sense of caring for each other and sharing good times and bad is evident in each selection.

Longfellow, Henry Wadsworth. *Paul Revere's Ride*. Illus. by Ted Rand. Dutton, 1990. The illustrations are true to the era the poem represents and offer young readers a sense of what it must have been like to ride through the countryside warning neighbors and fellow-patriots that dangerous evening.

Mahy, Margaret. *Nonstop Nonsense*. Illus. by Quentin Blake. Macmillan, 1989. Funny poems and short stories introduce a cast of eccentric characters. There is the wizard of words who casts a "spell" over the Delmonico family and the man from Fandango who visits once every 500 years.

Morrison, Lillian, compiler. *At the Crack of the Bat: Baseball Poems*. Illus. by Steve Cieslawski. Hyperion, 1992. The baseball season from spring training to the world series is celebrated in this collection. There are poems about Little League and famous major leaguers, about girls at bat and a day at the ballpark.

Opie, Iona and Peter. *I Saw Esau*. Illus. by Maurice Sendak. Candlewick, 1992. Schoolyard rhymes are here, from riddles and jump-rope chants to teasing insults. This is what children, through the ages, say to each other when adults are not listening. Sendak's roguish illustrations capture the essence of childhood.

Schwartz, Alvin. *And the Green Grass Grew All Around.* Illus. by Sue Truesdell. HarperCollins, 1992. A silly collection of rhymes sung in schoolyards and parks. The comical, scary, naughty poetry provokes laughter wherever children gather.

Silverstein, Shel. *Where the Sidewalk Ends.* Illus. by author. HarperCollins, 1974. Children who would not otherwise read poetry respond enthusiastically to these selections. Besides the humor, Silverstein pokes gentle fun at things children and their parents hold dear.

Soto, Gary. *Neighborhood Odes.* Illus. by David Diaz. HB, 1992. Celebrate life in a Mexican-American neighborhood with poems about tortillas and piñatas. Other poems about going to a wedding and watching a fireworks display are universal in their excitement.

Yolen, Jane, editor. *Street Rhymes Around the World.* Wordsong, 1992. Thirty-two rhymes chanted by children in seventeen countries as they play out in the street. Children's street games are universal as these rhymes from Brazil to as far as away as Armenia show us.

Dance

Barboza, Steven. *I Feel Like Dancing: A Year with Jacques d'Amboise and the National Dance Institute*. Photos by Carolyn George d'Amboise. Crown, 1992. D'Amboise, formerly a principal dancer with the New York City Ballet, travels to schools and introduces children to ballet. He spends a year preparing them for a spectacular performance, caught here in a delightful visual essay.

Dufort, Antony. *Ballet Steps: Practice to Performance*. Crown, 1990. Fans who enjoy watching ballet as well as ballet students appreciate the drawings and photographs of dancers as they go through their routines in preparation for a live ballet performance.

Fonteyn, Margot, adapter. *Swan Lake*. Illus. by Trina Schart Hyman. HB, 1989. The romantic legend of Prince Siegfried and Odette, his true love turned into a swan, is retold by one of the most famous ballerinas to ever dance the role of Odette.

Gregory, Cynthia. *Cynthia Gregory Dances Swan Lake*. Photos by Martha Swope. Simon & Schuster, 1990. The glamour of a prima ballerina's performance is dazzling, the accolade of fans is thrilling. Readers also see the endless round of grueling rehearsals and costume fittings amidst the glamour.

Krementz, Jill. *A Very Young Dancer*. Photos by author. Knopf, 1976. Hold your breath as Stephanie auditions for the lead role in the *Nutcracker* ballet. Follow her through grueling rehearsals and then onstage for the enchantment of her first performance.

Schick, Eleanor. *I Have Another Language, The Language Is Dance*. Illus. by author. Macmillan, 1992. A young ballerina discovers the joy of dancing is in communicating that joy to her audience, that performing involves a special interaction between dancer and viewer.

Streatfield, Noel. *Ballet Shoes*. Dent, 1936. A perennially popular story, the first in a series of novels about possible career choices, describes the training necessary to become a ballet dancer within the context of the story.

Werner, Vivian. *Petrouchka*. Illus. by John Collier. Viking, 1992. Petrouchka, a puppet clown, is held prisoner by the evil Magician who makes him dance while he longs to join the ballerina puppet he loves. Ballet fans cheer for Petrouchka's escape and efforts to unite the puppet lovers.

Folktales

Bader, Barbara. *Aesop & Company*. Illus. by Arthur Geisert. Houghton, 1991. Nineteen fables from 1,000 years ago uncover the truth about how we behave towards each other. Just as meaningful today, each fable has the moral of its story printed in bold type at the bottom of each page.

Chaucer, Geoffrey. *Canterbury Tales*. Selected, translated, and adapted by Barbara Cohen. Illus. by Trina Schart Hyman. Lothrop, 1988. Join the pilgrims on their way from London to Canterbury in 1386 and listen to the tales spun by four of the travelers to help pass the time. In turn they amuse, warn of greed, and poke fun at everyone.

Fairman, Tony. *Bury My Bones but Keep My Words*. Illus. by Meshack Asare. Holt, 1993. Stories collected from the length and breadth of Africa reflect many cultures, but all of them are full of the humor, life, and rhythm of their locale and are meant to be heard out loud.

Hodges, Margaret, adapter. *Saint George and the Dragon*. Illus. by Trina Schart Hyman. Little, Brown, 1984. The Queen of the Fairies sends the Red Cross Knight, later known as St. George, to battle the monstrous dragon who's terrorizing the countryside. He slays the dragon in heroic style and wins the hand of Princess Una. Jewel-toned illustrations enhance the drama.

Kipling, Rudyard. *Just So Stories*. Illus. by Safaya Salter. Holt, 1987. The leopard got his spots and the elephant got his trunk because that is what they deserved. The fate of the animals who lived by the "great-gray-green Limpopo river" is told with rare insight and much humor.

Lester, Julius. *How Many Spots Does a Leopard Have? And Other Tales*. Illus. by David Shannon. Scholastic, 1989. A collection of African and Jewish folktales depicting the universal character of human nature, making the stories seem like familiar old friends.

Osborne, Mary Pope. *American Tall Tales*. Illus. by Michael McCurdy. Knopf, 1991. Stories of nine legendary folk heroes are gathered in one volume. Best-loved tales of John Henry, Pecos Bill, Johnny Appleseed, and lots of others familiar for generations are collected for a new generation.

Scieszka, Jon. *The Stinky Cheese Man: And Other Fairly Stupid Tales*. Illus. by Lane Smith. Viking, 1992. For kids who think they're too old for traditional fairy tales this collection retells them as they might happen without the help of fairy godmothers: When the frog kisses the princess, her lips get slimy. The illustrations are equally unusual.

Walsh, Amanda. *The Buried Moon*. Houghton, 1991. The Moon hears that humans fear they will meet their death if they walk through a lonely bog on a moonless night, so she comes down from the sky leaving the world in darkness.

Our Developing Nation

Bial, Raymond. *County Fair*. Photos. Houghton, 1992. County fairs are as American as apple pie. Take a peek behind the scenes as crews prepare for opening day, set up exhibition tents, livestock pens, and rides; then meander along the midway on opening day.

Freedman, Russell. *The Wright Brothers: How They Invented the Airplane*. Photos by Orville and Wilbur Wright. Holiday, 1991. Follow the Wright brothers' descriptions of their theories and plans for building an airplane. Feel the excitement of early successful flights as well as the Wright's expectations for the commercial potential of flight.

Fritz, Jean. *Shh! We're Writing the Constitution*. Illus. by Tomie de Paola. Putnam, 1987. The Founding Fathers were real people who laughed, argued, disagreed, and finally cooperated to write the U.S. Constitution. Humorous details and personal anecdotes dramatize the events and draw readers back to that eventful era.

Haskins, Jim. *Get on Board: The Story of the Underground Railroad*. Scholastic, 1993.

Based on existing slave records, the story of the Underground Railroad is fascinating reading. The escape route to freedom with its stops along the way was more dangerous than modern readers can imagine.

Hilton, Suzanne. *A Capital Capitol City: 1790–1814.* Atheneum, 1993. An exciting account of the first twenty-four years of our nation's capitol, Washington, D.C., in which the city was sacked, burned, and rebuilt after the War of 1812, but always remained an electrifying place to be.

Jacobs, Francine. *The Tainos: The People Who Welcomed Columbus.* Illus. by Patrick Collins. Putnam, 1992. The friendly Tainos greeted Columbus when he sailed into the Caribbean and were seized as slaves, today they are extinct. Like a detective novel, clues to their culture are painstakingly uncovered.

Speare, Elizabeth George. *The Sign of the Beaver.* Houghton, 1983. Skeptical at first of Attean's offer of friendship, Matt learns to survive in the Maine wilderness during the late 1700s as the two boys come to appreciate each other's ways.

Stanley, Jerry. *Children of the Dust Bowl.* Crown, 1992. It is the 1930s and children of the Okie migrants have no school to attend. With their own hands they proudly help build the Weedpatch School and model farm where they learn a trade or prepare for college.

Uchida, Yoshiko. *The Invisible Thread*. Photos. Messner, 1992. This well-known author of children's books provides a look at her childhood, a study in contrasts. Her early years are spent in a happy Japanese-American home, then sudden internment in a prison camp at the outbreak of World War II.

Whitman, Sylvia. *V Is for Victory: The American Home Front During World War II*. Photos. Lerner, 1993. A war fought on foreign soil is felt at home. Food rationing, women going off to work, and the spirit and symbols of a nation united against a common enemy are news to a new generation of readers.

Discovering the World

Baird, Anne. *Space Camp: The Great Adventure for NASA Hopefuls*. Photos. Morrow, 1992. Follow twelve children through a week at a NASA Space Camp in Alabama as they build model rockets and test a variety of space equipment in preparation for a mock space flight.

Conrad, Pam. *Pedro's Journal*. Illus. by Peter Koeppen. Caroline House, 1991. A 500-year-old journal from Columbus's August 1492 voyage creates a feeling of sailing on that historic voyage. The excitement of seeing new sights and Pedro's concern for a safe journey home are entered in the journal.

Coville, Bruce. *Prehistoric People*. Illus. by Michael McDermott. Doubleday, 1990. The development of early man is told with great sensitivity and much excitement. Information on the evolution from gatherer to hunter to farmer is carefully presented as fact or identified as theory.

Demi. *Chingis Khan*. Illus. by author. Holt, 1991. Join the greatest army ever assembled up to the year 1206. Join the sweep across Asia, conquering everything along the way in the name of Chingis Khan, Emperor of Heaven.

Fraser, Mary Ann. *On Top of the World: The Conquest of Mount Everest*. Holt, 1991. The story of Sir Edmund Hillary and Tenzing Norgay's historic ascent of Mt. Everest in 1953 is as thrilling today as it was then. Readers see the careful planning that preceded the climb, ensuring its success.

Goodall, John S. *Great Days of a Country House*. Illus. by author. Macmillan, 1992. The world has changed dramatically over the last five centuries. These changes are reflected in the way one English country house has been altered to adapt to its residents' needs in each era. A stunning documentary.

Hautzig, Esther. *On the Air: Behind the Scenes*

at a TV Newscast. Photos by David Hautzig. Macmillan, 1991. Welcome to a TV news broadcast. Meet the newscasters and production staff as they describe their jobs. Go behind the scenes as stories are chosen for airing and prepared for broadcasting.

Hunt, Jonathan. *Illuminations.* Illus. by author. Bradbury, 1989. An ABC format and illustrations reminiscent of an illuminated manuscript bring the middle ages into sharp focus, transporting readers back in time.

Information, Please

Anno, Mitsumasa. *Anno's Medieval World.* Philomel, 1980. It is a time when most people believe the earth is flat and is the center of the universe. A few brave scientists dare to ask questions and make observation based on what they see in the heavens. Brave adventurers on the high seas set out to find the truth.

Ancona, George. *Turtle Watch.* Macmillan, 1987. A group of oceanographers enlist the children in a Brazilian village to help save endangered sea turtles.

Cole, Joanna. *The Magic School Bus on the Ocean Floor.* Illus. by Bruce Degen. Scholastic, 1992. Wacky Ms. Frizzle has done it again!

This time she takes her class to study the plants and animals living in the ocean's depths.

Cushman, Jean. *Do You Wanna Bet? Your Chance to Find Out about Probability.* Illus. by Martha Weston. Clarion, 1991. Two boys offer a light-hearted, brief discussion of probability, predicting, and sampling followed by examples of coin tossing, guessing games. breaking codes, and other probability chances. Readers are invited to predict the outcomes of various situations.

Downer, Ann. *Don't Blink Now! Capturing the Hidden World of Sea Creatures.* Watts, 1991. Close-up action photographs vividly show predatory sea creatures pursuing and catching other sea creatures. Other chapters emphasize survival and the future at the bottom of the sea.

Embury, Barbara. *The Dream Is Alive.* Photos. HarperCollins, 1990. Based on the Smithsonian/IMAX film of the same name, this is the story of shuttle flight. Readers learn how the astronauts eat in space and, of great interest to children, how they go to the bathroom.

Facklam, Margery. *Do Not Disturb: The Mysteries of Animal Hibernation and Sleep.* Illus. by Pamela Johnson. Sierra Club/Little, Brown, 1989. Different forms of hibernation, from deep sleep that lasts for months to brief periods of light sleep with lowered body temperature, are discussed. Examples are given of how scientists use beepers to monitor sleeping habits.

Lauber, Patricia. *Seeing Earth from Space.* Photos. Orchard, 1990. Breathtaking infrared photographs and radar imaging transmitted by satellite from space show scenes from around the world. The Grand Canyon appears like a livid scar cutting through Arizona.

Patent, Dorothy Hinshaw. *Looking at Dolphins and Porpoises.* Photos. Holiday, 1989. A close-up look at a variety of friendly sea creatures. How they are trained to perform at marine parks, live in families, and learn to communicate provide a fascinating glimpse of these mammals.

Pringle, Laurence. *Global Warming: Assessing the Greenhouse Threat.* Arcade, 1990. Using large print and a picture book format, a complex topic is calmly presented. Scientists' use of computer-based models to predict the effects of global warming is thoroughly explained.

Simon, Seymour. *Volcanoes.* Photos. Morrow, 1988. Using brilliant color photos Simon describes many types of volcanic activity and its positive effects on society.

Arnold, Caroline. *Soccer: From Neighborhood Play to the World Cup*. Watts, 1991. A complete guide to soccer in one volume. Rules, special equipment and skills are explained and youth soccer leagues are discussed. A section on competitive professional play rounds out the book.

Baillie, Marilyn. *Magic Fun*. Photos. Little, Brown, 1992. Kids are pictured performing magic tricks that really work and which they can do on their own. Easy to follow step-by-step directions are given along with a scientific explanation.

Blum, Raymond. *Mathemagic*. Illus. by Jeff Sinclair. Sterling, 1992. Learn tricks, magic, and other math-based activities to impress friends and family. All that is needed is a simple hand-held calculator, a deck of cards, or a pencil; the puzzles cover a wide range of math ability.

Brown, Fern G. *Special Olympics*. Photos. Watts, 1992. The history of the Special Olympics for developmentally and physically challenged young people from its origin in 1963, along with stories of some of the participants, is inspiring reading.

Churchill, E. Richard. *Fabulous Paper Airplanes*. Illus. by James Michaels. Sterling, 1991. Always a popular activity, easy to follow instructions are given for building 29 paper airplanes. Most only require a single sheet of paper but some advanced designs require clips, straws, or other household materials.

Cooper, Michael L. *Playing America's Game: The Story of Negro League Baseball*. Photos. Dutton, 1993. Major Negro league ballplayers are featured, along with information about their teams and the racism players had to endure.

Dowd, Ned. *That's a Wrap: How Movies Are Made*. Simon & Schuster, 1991. Go behind the scenes with Dowd, a film producer, for a dramatic, exciting experience. Learn about the different jobs on a movie set and the people who do them, then see the equipment used to shoot various scenes.

Friedhoffer, Robert. *Magic Tricks, Science Facts*. Illus. by Richard Kaufman. Watts, 1990. Anyone can become a master magician. Methods, materials needed, and the scientific principle guiding the magic are all carefully explained and accompanied by a photo and diagram. A sure fire hit!

Frommer, Harvey. *Baseball's Hall of Fame*. Photos. Watts, 1985. The lives of fifty of the most famous baseball players enshrined at the Cooperstown Hall of Fame are briefly sketched.

Golenbock, Peter. *Teammates*. Illus. by Paul Bacon. Gulliver/HB, 1990. It's 1947 and the

Brooklyn Dodgers are about to win the pennant. Will the new player be allowed on the field? With a smile and a clasped shoulder, star shortstop Pee Wee Reese welcomes Jackie Robinson, the first black player to integrate the major leagues. With rare vintage photos.

Lasker, Joe. *A Tournament of Knights*. Illus. by author. HarperCollins, 1986. Before there was baseball there was jousting. Play at a tournament of knights with Justin, a baron's son, in the Middle Ages. The weight and heat of his armor are almost too much to bear but the feasting afterwards is memorable.

McGraw, Sheila. *Papier-Mâché for Kids*. Firefly Books, 1991. Clear instructions are given for making and decorating bracelets, masks, and six other projects. Instructions and materials are clearly stated in a box at the start of each project.

Thayer, Ernest Lawrence. *Casey at the Bat*. Illus. by Barry Moser. Godine, 1988. It's Mudville, U.S.A. in 1888 and Mighty Casey steps up to bat. The game was as exciting then as it is now whenever fans wait for one superstar to save the day.

Jokes and Riddles

Gale, David, editor. *Funny You Should Ask: The Delacorte Book of Original Humorous Short*

Stories. Delacorte, 1992. Instead of one-line jokes the humor is extended to a collection of short stories by outstanding children's book authors.

Hall, Godfrey. *Mind Twisters*. Random House, 1991. For any child who has ever wanted to build a jet engine, create a secret code, learn the secret of optical illusions, and other number tricks and puzzles.

Juster, Norton. *A Surfeit Of Similes*. Illus. by David Small. Morrow, 1989. Humorous illustrations and a slightly offbeat collection of comparisons guaranteed to make readers smile as they learn to use similes to enhance their own writing.

Maestro, Giulio. *More Halloween Howls: Riddles That Come Back to Haunt You*. Dutton, 1992. "Rice-Creepies" and "Croaker Cola" provoke belly laughs among the book's intended audience. The jokes and riddles are right on target for this age group.

Phillips, Louis. *Wackysaurus: Dinosaur Jokes*. Illus. by Ron Barrett. Viking, 1991. The humor depends on riddles, jokes, and wordplay that leaves children begging for more, while adults are left groaning.

Smith, William Jay. *Behind the King's Kitchen*. Illus. by Jacques Hnizdovsky. Wordsong, 1992. A collection of over 150 riddles, all written in rhyme, to tickle the funnybone and stump the reader.

Terban, Marvin. *Funny You Should Ask*. Illus. by John O'Brien. Clarion, 1992. Wordplay jokes based on sound-alike words and expressions strike a funny chord in young readers. They also receive pointers on making up their own jokes and riddles to trick friends and unsuspecting parents.

Terban, Marvin. *Hey, Hay! A Wagonful of Funny Homonym Riddles*. Illus. by Kevin Hawkes. Clarion, 1991. Wordplay, mayhem, and nonsense reign even as riddles rain down on readers offering new twists on familiar words and expressions. The illustrations are as silly as the riddles.

Chapter 11

Eleven and Twelve Year Olds

Sports, Hobbies, Action

Andersen, Yvonne. *Make Your Own Animated Movies and Videotapes.* Little, Brown, 1991. Directions for working alone or with a group enable readers to create videotape and computer animation, clay animation, and other forms of up-to-the-minute animation.

Platt, Richard. *Incredible Cross-Sections.* Illus. by Stephen Biesty. Knopf, 1992. See inside buildings and machines in intimate, detailed drawings to learn how the Empire State building was constructed, how a jumbo jet is designed, how the Queen Mary was built, and the list of cross-sections goes on.

Brooks, Bruce. *The Moves Make the Man.* HarperCollins, 1984. Jayfox and Bix practice the moves needed to become star basketball players. What's tougher is Jayfox's experience as the first black student to integrate the junior high and Bix's experience having to cope with the absence of his mother, who is away in an institution.

Cushman, Kathleen, and Montana Miller. *Circus Dreams: The Making Of a Circus Artist.* Photos by Michael Carroll. Little, Brown, 1989. Spend one year with Montana Miller as she trains intensively to become a trapeze artist. Share her fear, her anticipation, and the final glory of performing.

Duder, Tessa. *In Lane Three, Alex Archer.* Houghton, 1989. Alex is close to being chosen one of two girls to represent New Zealand in the Olympics. The pressure is great and she is driven to succeed as she learns to control her strokes and her emotions.

Kettlekamp. Larry. *Computer Graphics: How It Works, What It Does.* Morrow, 1989. In concise, clear language graphic imaging systems are explained and examples of actual applications, such as music composing and drawing maps, are given.

Lewis, Brenda Ralph. *Stamps!* Lodestar, 1991. An oversized book with colorful illustrations useful for beginners getting started collecting stamps. The history of postage stamps from around the world and how they have come to be valued as works of art are highlighted.

Perl, Lila. *The Great Ancestor Hunt.* Illus. by

Erika Weihs. Clarion, 1989. An unusual how-to book: all the "ingredients" needed to find long-lost ancestors and places of origin are here, ready to be investigated.

Schmitt, Lois. *Smart Spending: A Young Consumer's Guide.* Scribner's, 1989. For readers interested in knowing how to spend their money wisely, live on a budget, and evaluate misleading advertising. Real-life examples are used to illustrate ways of becoming a savvy consumer.

Severn, Bill. *Magic Fun for Everyone.* Illus. by Fred Kraus. Dutton, 1986. Features magic tricks that can be done with everyday materials. Diagrams and instructions are helpful in preparing the tricks and being comfortable when perfoming.

Soto, Gary. *Baseball in April and Other Stories.* HB, 1990. Michael and Jesse, brothers in the title story in this collection, try their hardest to make the Little League team. These eleven short stories feature Mexican-American youngsters in California.

Tunis, John R. *The Kid from Tompkinsville.* HB/Odyssey Classics, 1948, 1968. Ray Tucker's pitching career with the Brooklyn Dodgers is abruptly ended when he has a freak accident. Coming to terms with his new life provides the basis for this classic sports story.

Wallechinsky, David. *The Complete Book of the Olympics.* Viking, 1988. Brief summaries of the most exciting Olympic competitions are included along with complete results of events at all winter and summer games.

Our Developing Nation

Ashabranner, Brent. *Born to the Land.* Photos by Paul Conklin. Putnam, 1989. The American cowboy and farmer are romantic figures in settling the West. Here they tell, in their own words, how the pioneer image exists today alongside the reality of modern technology.

Blumberg, Rhoda. *The Great American Gold Rush.* Bradbury, 1989. People rushed overland and by sea to make their fortunes during the Gold Rush. Living conditions were brutal, justice was harsh, and few became rich, as this documentary book shows.

Fisher, Leonard Everett. *Ellis Island.* Photos. Holiday, 1986. Fifteen million immigrants passed through Ellis Island between 1892 and 1954. Here are the stories of many people's relatives; the hopes for success, the fears of being sent back.

Freedman, Russell. *Indian Chiefs.* Holiday, 1987. Illustrated with historical photos and drawings, the settling of the western frontier is viewed from the perspective of six Indian chiefs including Sitting Bull and Chief Joseph.

Freedman, Russell. *Lincoln: A Photobiography.* Clarion, 1987. Lots of first-person source material lets Lincoln speak for himself in his own words. Lively anecdotes from friends and family round out the picture of a real person, not a legendary one.

Fritz, Jean. *The Great Little Madison.* Putnam, 1989. Despite his small stature and tiny speaking voice, Madison conveyed great passion. His feud with the overpowering Patrick Henry went in Madison's favor as did his love for the beautiful Dolley Madison.

Hamanaka, Sheila. *The Journey: Japanese Americans, Racism, and Renewal.* Illus. by author. Orchard, 1990. Paintings by the author show the horror in the Japanese-American community during World War II when they were taken from their homes and communities and resettled in barren internment camps.

Jenness, Aylette, and Alice Rivers. *In Two Worlds: A Yup'ik Eskimo Family.* Houghton, 1989. Alice Rivers and her family enjoy many modern conveniences while maintaining their Eskimo culture. Her sons learn to hunt and fish as their grandfathers did, everyone enjoys Eskimo food and traditions.

Johnston, Norma. *Louisa May.* Photos. Four

Winds, 1991. Louisa May Alcott, author of *Little Women*, turned to writing in the late 19th century because so few career opportunities were available to women. She was a creative woman with an unsentimental outlook on life, able to accomplish her goals.

Macaulay, David. *Underground.* Illus. by author. Houghton, 1976. A view of the underground structures that hold skyscrapers and cities together. This also explains how water, sewer, communications, and transportation services are delivered by cities to their residents.

McKissack, Patricia, and Fredrick McKissack. *A Long Hard Journey.* Walker, 1989. Former slaves and their sons fight for the right to organize the first black labor union, the Brotherhood of Sleeping Car Porters, in 1925. Their struggles, successes, and folklore are all here.

Meltzer, Milton. *Columbus and the World Around Him.* Watts, 1990. Drawn from his ship's logs and other firsthand accounts, a picture of Columbus as an insensitive dreamer seeking fabulous treasures and confident he'd found the eastern coast of Asia, emerges.

St. George, Judith. *Panama Canal: Gateway to the World.* Photos. Putnam, 1989. The ten-year struggle to hack through jungle, swamp, and mountains to connect the Atlantic and Pacific Oceans takes an enormous toll in human life even as a cure for yellow fever is found.

Taylor, Mildred. *Roll of Thunder, Hear My Cry.* Dial, 1976. Cassie Logan is determined and proud of her black heritage. She and her brothers set out to help the family keep their land and remain independent despite the obstacles prejudice puts in their path in Mississippi during the Depression. Other titles about Cassie and the Logans include *Let the Circle Be Unbroken* and *The Friendship.*

Murphy, Jim. *The Boys' War: Confederate and Union Soldiers Talk About the Civil War.* Photos. Clarion, 1990. Diaries, letters, and journals are used to tell about the experiences of young Civil War soldiers. Boys as young as thirteen spare no detail of what they witness as their lives are forever changed.

Other Lives, Other Worlds

Ballard, Robert D. *Exploring the Titanic: How the Greatest Ship Ever Lost Was Found.* Illus. by Ken Marschall. Scholastic, 1988. Ballard and his robot, Jason, dive to the ocean's depths to explore and photograph the hulk of the *Titanic.* Jason descends the ship's grand staircase to photograph the exquisite chandeliers.

Blumberg, Rhoda. *The Remarkable Voyages of Captain Cook.* Bradbury, 1991. Sail around the world with Captain Cook on his quest for an unknown continent. Brave cruel weather and cannibals with the crew as Cook searches for the Northwest Passage and finds the warmth of the South Pacific.

Gordon, Sheila. *Waiting for the Rain.* Orchard, 1987. Confronted with the stereotypes of racial prejudice, two friends, one black and one white, face the reality of the segregation laws in South Africa. Their friendship is torn apart as one friend enters the military and one stays in school.

Hoffman, Yair. *The World of the Bible for Young Readers.* Illus. by Ilana Shamir. Viking, 1989. Each chapter explains a period and area of Middle Eastern history beginning with Canaan and the Fertile Crescent through the beginnings of Christianity. The full-color illustrations are stunning.

Rogasky, Barbara. *Smoke and Ashes: The Story of the Holocaust.* Photos. Holiday, 1988. An up-close look at the extermination of more than six million Jews in Europe during World War II. Its causes, events, and legacies are discussed and related to other instances of intolerance in the world today.

Sancha, Sheila. *Walter Dragun's Town.* Illus. by author. Crowell, 1989. Spend a week in a medieval town, work at spinning cloth or making metal bowls and swords. Attend the annual trade fair, a tournament of knights, and greet the king's justices as they come to inspect the town of Stanford in 1275.

Stanley, Diane, and Peter Vennema. *Bard of Avon: The Story of William Shakespeare.* Illus. by Diane Stanley. Morrow, 1992. Experience life in the Elizabethan age as a member of Shakespeare's Globe Theatre company. Spend time with the cast, then retire to the country with Shakespeare.

Science Fiction and High Fantasy

Adams, Douglas. *The Hitchhiker's Guide to the Galaxy.* Pocket Books, 1980. Arthur Dent, armed with his intergalactic guidebook, escapes when he hears that earth is about to be demolished to make way for an intergalactic highway. There are several other titles in this series.

Bradbury, Ray. *R Is for Rocket.* Bantam, 1962. Seventeen short stories about monsters, time travel, life on Venus and Mars, and all kinds of situations so scary they're best not read alone. This and other titles by Bradbury defy all recent scientific developments.

Christopher, John. *The White Mountains.* Macmillan, 1967; Collier, 1970. Will Parker and his friends attempt a desperate escape to the White Mountains to avoid being capped by the interplanetary Tripods seeking to control their thoughts and behavior in a future world. *The City of Gold and Lead* and *The Pool of Fire* are exciting sequels to this mind-control fantasy series.

Doyle, Arthur Conan. *The Adventures of Sherlock Holmes.* Illus. by Barry Moser. Morrow, 1992. Twelve classic mystery adventures of the fictional detective, Sherlock Holmes, and his trusty companion, Dr. Watson, in a newly illustrated edition.

Gilmore, Kate. *Enter Three Witches.* Houghton, 1990. Bren has more than his school production of Macbeth to worry about. His mother, grandmother, and their boarder, witches all, are coming to the play and offer help with special effects.

Griffiths, Barbara. *Frankenstein's Hamster: Ten Spine-Tingling Tales.* Dial, 1992. Each story is terrifying in its own way, from the story set in an Egyptian tomb to the story where pet cats bare their teeth ready to attack their owners. Not for the gentle-hearted.

Jones, Diana Wynne. *Howl's Moving Castle.* Greenwillow, 1986. Sophie Hatter, turned into an ugly old woman by the Wicked Witch of the Waste, becomes embroiled in a feud between

Wizard Howl and the Witch when she hides out in Howl's moving castle where she works as his housekeeper.

Klause, Annete Curtis. *The Silver Kiss*. Delacorte, 1990. Zoe has a host of personal problems to confront but meeting Simon changes everything. Simon is a vampire searching through time to find his brother and kill him, but he needs a taste of blood to keep him going.

McCaffrey, Anne. *Dragonflight*. Ballantine, 1978. Complete with dragons and intergalactic threats of war, this series about the inhabitants of Pern is perennially popular with young readers.

Mahy, Margaret. *The Changeover: A Supernatural Romance*. Atheneum, 1984. An evil wizard possesses Laura's brother and she is powerless to help him. An appeal to her friend Sorenson enlists his mother and grandmother, both witches, in the delicate task of transmitting supernatural power to Laura.

Raskin, Ellen. *The Westing Game*. Dutton, 1978. Try to figure out the clues and guess the answer encoded in a mysterious will. The clues are based on offbeat plays on words, cunning tricks, and disguises.

Schwartz, Alvin. *Scary Stories to Tell in the Dark*. Illus. by Stephen Gammell. HarperCollins, 1983. This collection of tales of the supernatural is guaranteed to set the reader's teeth on edge. Children enjoy reading them aloud to friends, brothers, and sisters, trying to scare each other.

Sleator, William. *The Duplicate.* Dutton, 1988. David wishes he can be in two places at once and with a machine that duplicates organic matter he can. Things are fine until his clone makes a duplicate of himself. Then David's troubles really begin.

Voigt, Cynthia. *Jackaroo.* Atheneum, 1985. Set in a mythical time and place, Gwyn, a teen-aged girl assumes the role of Jackaroo, a Robin Hood-style character, when she finds Jackaroo's costume in a deserted cabin. Her swashbuckling adventures continue in *On Fortune's Wheel* (1990).

Science Fact

Berger, Melvin. *The Science of Music.* Crowell, 1989. Why do we hear different sounds from different instruments, some louder, some softer? Keyboard, brass, wind, and percussion instruments are all explained as well as how the new electronic instruments work.

Cowing, Sheila. *Searches in the American Desert.* Photos by Walter C. Cowing. Macmillan, 1989. The searches of eight American adventurers center around the quest for treasure, for a religious haven, and for peace through atomic energy. They all found gila monsters and other natural wonders of the desert.

Dowden, Anne Ophelia. *The Clover & the Bee: A Book of Pollination.* Illus. by the author. Crowell, 1990. The contribution of flowers and the animals who make pollination possible is exciting when seen as a partnership in the chain of life. Color drawings of the flowers are exquisite.

Downer, John. *Supersense: Perception in the Animal World.* Photos by author. Holt, 1989. At the first sign of an earthquake, before people are aware or seismographs give any indication, animals sense trouble and scurry for cover. Read why animals are sensitive to atmospheric change and other phenomena.

Johnson, Rebecca. *The Greenhouse Effect: Life on a Warmer Planet.* Lerner, 1990. The effects of carbon dioxide pollution in the atmosphere is given as the chief cause of global warming. While avoiding sensationalism, suggestions are given for what individual readers can do to help.

Johnson, Sylvia A. *Roses Red, Violets Blue: Why Flowers Have Colors.* Photos by Yuko Sato. Lerner, 1991. People enjoy the beautiful range of colors in flowers. But color, for a flower, is more significant than just being pretty, flower color affects plants' functions.

Kelch, Joseph W. *Small Worlds: Exploring the*

60 Moons of Our Solar System. Photos. Messner, 1990. Descriptions of the 60 known moons in our solar system are based on what scientists have recently learned from flights of the Voyager spacecraft.

Lasky, Kathryn. *Surtsey: The Newest Place on Earth.* Photos by Christopher G. Knight. Hyperion, 1992. Attend the birth of an island: It is 1963, near Iceland in the north Atlantic Ocean when fire erupts. The island of Surtsey emerges and readers observe the emergence of simple life-forms.

Lauber, Patricia. *Voyagers from Space: Meteors and Meteorites.* Illus. by Mike Eagle. Crowell, 1989. The Donahue family sits at home watching TV when rocks crash through their walls. A meteorite is lying under the table. Lauber explains about meteorites and what the chances are of this happening again.

Macaulay, David. *The Way Things Work.* Illus. by author. Houghton, 1988. From simple mechanical inventions such as the screw and lever through can openers and parking meters to sophisticated flight simulators and microprocessors, Macaulay patiently and humorously explains it all. A masterpiece for all ages.

Patent, Dorothy Hinshaw. *How Smart Are Animals?* HB, 1990. How smart do you think your pet puppy or cat is? Read about ways scientists try to determine animal intelligence and how animals think. Some of the animals included are dolphins, sea lions, gorillas, birds, and humans, too.

Skurzynski, Gloria. *Almost the Real Thing: Simulation in Your High-Tech World.* Bradbury, 1981. Astronauts train for space flight and crash and earthquake resistant materials are tested through computer simulated situations. Find out how scientists and engineers use computer animation, weightlessness, and similar technologies to study real-life situations and prepare for them.

Poetry

Agard, John, compiler. *Life Doesn't Frighten Me At All.* Holt, 1990. In a volume small enough to tuck into a backpack readers discover eighty-four poems from around the world, not likely to be found in other collections. There are traditional poets and others such as Bob Marley, the reggae artist.

An Illustrated Treasury of Songs. Rizzoli, 1991. Fifty-five tried-and-true songs — with words and music — for glorious singing along. There are patriotic songs, songs to sing at parties and around the campfire: "Clementine" to "I've Been Working on the Railroad."

Coleridge, Samuel Taylor. *The Rime of the Ancient Mariner.* Illus. by Ed Young. Atheneum,

1992. This oversized volume shows a small ship sailing on the vast ocean, suggesting the forlorn loneliness of the mariner. The albatross first appears as a small bird; in the shipwreck scene narrative it flies away with immense outstretched wings.

Fleischman, Paul. *Joyful Noise: Poems for Two Voices.* Illus. by Eric Beddows. HarperCollins, 1988. Meant for two or more voices to read together, these humorous poems tell about insects and how they survive their daily lives.

Glenn, Mel. *Back to Class.* Photos by Michael J. Bernstein. Clarion, 1988. High school students in these poems tell their own stories about growing up, having friends, and getting along with their parents and teachers.

Goldstein, Bobbye, selector. *Inner Chimes.* Illus. by Jane Breskin Zalben. Wordsong, 1992. An anthology of poems about poetry and the words and rhymes that shape the writer's thoughts into poetry. Some poems tell about the inspiration that led to their creation.

Janeczko, Paul B, editor. *The Place My Words Are Looking For.* Bradbury, 1990. Poems by thirty-nine American authors as well as their thoughts on how to write poetry will help budding writers get started. They offer encouragement and sympathetic advice that is easy to take.

Janeczko, Paul B, selector. *Preposterous: Poems*

of Youth. Orchard, 1991. More than 100 short poems by popular authors focus on youth and the experiences of growing up. Many are light-hearted but they all deal with themes and emotions young readers care deeply about.

Morrison, Lillian, compiler. *Sprints and Distances: Sports In Poetry and the Poetry In Sport.* Crowell, 1989. Some are funny, some seriously describe the terrors of competition. But this collection of poems covers every sport possible, including kite flying.

Morrison, Lillian, compiler. *Yours till Niagara Falls: A Book of Autograph Verses.* Illus. by Sylvie Wickstrom. Crowell, 1990. There are over 200 funny, silly, and sentimental rhymes by kids to help readers decide what to write in friends' yearbooks and autograph albums.

Nye, Naomi Shihab, compiler. *This Same Sky: A Collection of Poems from Around the World.* Four Winds, 1992. Poetry from all over the world is universal in the emotions represented. Poets care about each other and the wonders of nature; they worry about the environment, natural and political.

Rylant, Cynthia. *Soda Jerk.* Illus. by Pete Catalanotto. Orchard, 1990. From his vantage behind the soda fountain the narrator gets to hear everyone's story. He tells us about teenagers and lonely old ladies who come for a soda but really to talk.

Hopkins, Lee Bennett, editor. *Rainbows Are Made: Poems by Carl Sandburg.* Illus. by Fritz Eichenberg. HB, 1982. A selection of poems taken from several of Carl Sandburg's books. Some honor the American experience settling the land, most express universal feelings, and all reflect Sandburg's wry sense of humor.

Survival Stories

Cole, Brock. *The Goats.* FS&G, 1987. Stripped naked and left on a small island by their fellow campers, a boy and girl find the inner resources to survive and the confidence to believe in themselves and trust each other.

Conrad, Pam. *Prairie Songs.* Illus. by Darryl Zudeck. HarperCollins, 1985. Life is harsh on the Nebraska prairie at the turn of the century. Louisa watches her mother flourish while her neighbor's frail wife, Emmeline, loses her determination to survive.

George, Jean. *Julie of the Wolves.* HarperCollins, 1972. Julie, known by her Inuit name of Miyax, is lost in the Arctic tundra. With winter approaching her only hope of survival is to be accepted by a pack of wolves.

Houston, Jeanne Wakatsuki. *Farewell to Manzanar.* Houghton, 1973. The author recounts her Japanese-American family's internment behind barbed wire during World War II. Despite meager efforts to relieve the indignities of camp life, she witnessed many surrender their hope and not survive.

Hudson, Jan. *Sweetgrass.* Philomel, 1984. Sweetgrass is sure that she is mature enough to marry the Blackfoot warrior, Eagle-Sun. Not until she fights for her family's survival, during the 1838 smallpox outbreak that ravaged her tribe, does she earn the right to accept Eagle-Sun's gift of horses.

Hurmence, Belinda. *A Girl Called Boy.* Clarion, 1982. Nicknamed Boy, an 11-year-old girl is transported back to the era of slavery. She lives the horrors of slavery and survives an effort to escape before returning to modern times and her family.

Murphy, Claire Rudolf. *To the Summit.* Dutton, 1992. Sarah is determined to climb Mt. McKinley, the highest peak in North America. She trains hard only to discover more than physical stamina is needed for success.

O'Dell, Scott. *Island of the Blue Dolphins.* Houghton, 1960. When their tribe is forcibly removed from their Pacific island, Karana and her brother are sure they will be rescued. Her brother dies and Karana survives alone for eighteen years. Based on a true account of Karana's ordeal. An unforgettable story.

Orlev, Uri. *The Man from the Other Side.* Houghton, 1991. Marek and his stepfather trudge through the slime of Warsaw's sewers to deliver food to inmates of the Warsaw Ghetto during World War II. As the uprising starts, Marek manages to help some partisans escape back through the sewers.

Paulsen, Gary. *The River.* Delacorte, 1991. Brian Robeson, the hero of *Hatchet*, is on a camping trip in the Canadian wilderness when his companion, Derek, is struck by lightning. Brian must tame the river rapids to haul Derek 100 miles for the nearest help. An exciting and gripping tale.

Yep, Laurence. *Dragonwings.* HarperCollins, 1975. At the turn of the century, Moon Shadow leaves China to join Windrider, his father, in San Francisco's Chinatown. Facing racial prejudice and the San Francisco earthquake, Windrider survives by keeping his dream of flying alive.

Growing Up

Avi. *Nothing But the Truth.* Orchard, 1992. It starts with a failing grade that keeps Philip from joining the track team and ends when everyone in school, in town, and on the national news take sides in what appears to be a freedom of speech issue.

Blume, Judy. *Just As Long As We're Together.* Orchard, 1987. Stephanie thinks she has enough to deal with trying to sort out her parent's recent separation and meeting her dad's new friend, Iris, until her best friend, Rachel, includes a newcomer in their friendship.

Brooks, Bruce. *What Hearts.* HarperCollins, 1992. Four stories about Asa revolve around his development as a ballplayer and his relationship with his mother and stepfather. Asa learns success as a ballplayer is as difficult as growing up.

Byars, Betsy. *Bingo Brown and the Language of Love.* Viking, 1989. Bingo's worries about facing his growing responsibilities and awakening interest in girls are met head on and handled with sympathy and humor.

Crew, Linda. *Children of the River.* Delacorte, 1989. To keep alive the customs and values her family brought from Asia, while fitting comfortably into school life, becomes a problem for Sundara, a Cambodian immigrant.

Duncan, Lois. *I Know What You Did Last Summer.* Little, Brown, 1973. Four good friends have a dark secret to keep about a hit-and-run accident that caused the death of a little boy. Only now someone else has learned their secret and is trying to get revenge.

Dygard, Thomas. *Backfield Package.* Morrow, 1992. Joe and his best friends, stars of their high school team, are determined to play football together in college. But only Joe is offered a scholarship to play for a school with a major football team.

Hobbs, Will. *Bearstone*. Atheneum, 1989. Cloyd finds a small turquoise bear when he is sent by his tribe to help an old rancher for the summer. He hopes the bear will keep him company in his loneliness but finds much more instead.

Lasky, Kathryn. *The Bone Wars*. Morrow, 1988. Thad works as a scout in the Montana Badlands in the late 1800s and gets to meet General Custer and Sitting Bull. When he and a friend uncover dinosaur remains, deciding what to do with them becomes a problem.

McKinley, Robin. *Beauty: A Retelling of the Story of Beauty and the Beast*. HarperCollins, 1978. An expanded retelling of the classic fairy tale where Beauty finds her own strength and makes her own decisions.

Myers, Walter Dean. *Scorpions*. HarperCollins, 1988. Resisting the temptations of street life in Harlem is a tough challenge for Jamal. When he is pressured to take over his jailed brother's gang, Jamal narrowly avoids tragedy.

Nixon, Joan Lowery. *A Deadly Promise*. Bantam/ Starfire, 1992. Sarah spends the last few moments with her father before his death and makes him a promise. In this sequel to *High*

Trail to Danger, Sarah and her sister attempt to solve the mystery of her promise and restore her father's honor.

Okimoto, Jean Davies. *Molly By Any Other Name*. Scholastic, 1990. Molly, an Asian-American high school senior, contacts the Northwest Adoptees Search Organization to begin the search for her birth mother.

Paterson, Katherine. *Jacob Have I Loved*. Crowell, 1980. Louise believes her self-centered twin sister Caroline is, unfairly, the favored child. As she learns to let go of her bitterness, Louise finds her place among the Chesapeake Bay fishermen and her own place in the world.

Rylant, Cynthia. *Missing May*. Orchard, 1992. Twelve-year-old Summer and her uncle, Ob, have a hard time when Aunt May dies. Accompanied by one of Summer's classmates, they leave on a trip and learn to live with their grief in the process.

Silver, Norman. *No Tigers in Africa*. Dutton, 1992. Selwyn is recently arrived in England from South Africa. He is haunted by the memory that he helped cause the death of a black teenager back home and cannot find a way to live with his guilt.

White, Ryan. *Ryan White: My Own Story*. Dial, 1991. The autobiography of a 13-year-old who contracted AIDS as a hemophiliac describes his courageous battle as a spokesperson for people with AIDS.

Zindel, Paul. *The Pigman*. HarperCollins, 1968. Lorraine and John make friends with elderly Mr. Pignati, the Pigman as they call him. While he is in the hospital they use his house for a party with disastrous consequences.

Animal and Nature Stories

Arnosky, Jim. *Secrets of a Wildlife Watcher*. Illus. by author. Lothrop, 1983. The author's delight in nature and wildlife creatures is conveyed through his attention to detail as he explains his wildlife watching techniques and comments on his observations.

Burnford, Sheila. *The Incredible Journey*. Illus. by Carl Burger. Little, Brown, 1961. Two dogs and a Siamese cat undertake a 250-mile life-threatening trek through the Canadian wilderness trying to find their way back home. These house pets fend off larger animals, well-meaning humans, and cruel weather.

Dolan, Edward F., Jr. *Animal Rights*. Photos. Watts, 1986. Do animals have rights? Are they the same as rights for people? Starting with these questions a discussion ensues on how to promote humane treatment of animals while recognizing their historic contributions to civilization.

George, Jean. *My Side of the Mountain*. Dutton, 1959. Sam Gribley survives a year living in the hollow trunk of a tree. He records in his diary that cattails should be well-cooked before eating and how he captured his pet falcon, Frightful.

Gipson, Fred. *Old Yeller*. Illus. by Carl Burger. HarperCollins, 1956. Travis has enough responsibility on his family's ranch while his father is away herding cattle; he resents the arrival of the old yellow dog. Slowly, Old Yeller wins his affection as he protects the family from raiding wolves, bears, and other dangers.

Herriot, James. *All Creatures Great and Small*. Bantam, 1972. A veterinarian practicing in the English countryside reminisces about his experiences in a gentle, humorous tone. He cares for all kinds of household and farm animals and, sometimes, attends to their owners.

Loeper, John J. *Crusade for Kindness: Henry Bergh and the ASPCA*. Atheneum, 1991. Unsanitary conditions exist in slaughterhouses and animals are worked until they drop in the late 1800s. Henry Bergh crusades for humane treatment of animals and is ridiculed until he founds the ASPCA.

Lourie, Peter. *Hudson River*. Photos. Caroline

House, 1992. Start in the Adirondack Mountains, at the source of the Hudson River, and sail by canoe to the tip of Manhattan where the Hudson empties into the Atlantic Ocean. Paddle past farms, old industrial mills, and a modern nuclear power plant along the way.

Patent, Dorothy Hinshaw. *Where the Bald Eagles Gather*. Photos by William Munoz. Clarion, 1984. The work of the wildlife tracking project that is monitoring the life cycle of our endangered national symbol, the bald eagle, is described. Photographs capture their annual gathering at Glacier National Park.

Paulsen, Gary. *Woodsong*. Illus. by Ruth Paulsen. Bradbury, 1990. The author of *Hatchet* and *Canyons* writes about his experience racing in the Iditarod dogsled race in Alaska. The bond that develops between him and his team of dogs is intense and mysterious, while he is ever mindful that the dogs are wild animals.

Pringle, Laurence. *Animals at Play*. HB, 1985. Photos show several familiar animals, from cats and dogs to bats, wolves, and monkeys, at play. Scientific evidence is presented explaining why it is as important for animals to play as it is for children.

Mummies and the Ancient World

Cohen, Daniel. *The Tomb Robbers*. McGraw-

Hill, 1980. How the robbery of buried treasure from ancient tombs, not a mummy's curse, interferes with efforts to study ancient civilizations and the process of mummification.

Connolly, Peter. *The Roman Fort.* Illus. by author. Oxford, 1991. Excavation of a fort near Hadrian's Wall in England reveals living quarters and other buildings, permitting a picture of the lives of ordinary soldiers and their commanders to emerge.

Giblin, James Cross. *The Riddle of the Rosetta Stone: Key to Ancient Egypt.* Photos. Crowell, 1990. The key to deciphering the code of ancient Egyptian hieroglyphics by Napoleon's army, scholars, and fools reads like a fast-paced detective novel.

Goor, Ron and Nancy Goor. *Pompeii: Exploring a Roman Ghost Town.* Crowell, 1986. When Mt. Vesuvius erupted in 79 A.D. the city of Pompeii was destroyed but perfectly preserved. Text and photos let the reader look at people as they went about their everyday lives in ancient times.

Lauber, Patricia. *Tales Mummies Tell.* Crowell, 1985. The latest scientific techniques are used to uncover the secrets of mummies. Bones are reconstructed and teeth examined to discover ancient diets and life-styles.

Macaulay, David. *Pyramid.* Illus. by author. Houghton, 1975. The process of building a pyramid from drawing plans to setting the huge granite blocks in place is explained in detailed text and illustrations. Macaulay also provides information and illustration showing how mummies were prepared and placed in the pyramids.

Meyer, Carolyn, and Charles Gallenkamp. *The Mystery of the Ancient Maya*. Atheneum. 1985. Why did the ancient Maya civilization flourish and then disappear in Central America? Read about the unsolved mysteries of the Maya and their advances in mathematics and agriculture that surpassed their European contemporaries.

Reeves, Nicholas. *Into the Mummy's Tomb*. Scholastic, 1992. Explore the mystery, discover the secret cache that only the butler knew about King Tut's tomb.

Sattler, Helen Roney. *Hominids: A Look Back at Our Ancestors*. Illus. by Christopher Santoro. Lothrop, 1988. Anthropologists analyze the tiniest clues then string them together to solve the mystery surrounding the daily life of prehistoric people.

A Personal Note

When I come to the end of a manuscript, I think about the promise and hope that goes out with a book. Perhaps because I grew up on a farm I think of planting seeds, nurturing crops and readers, fertilizing the soil, making the environment rich, and keeping the world a healthy place for our children. Perhaps because the breath of spring is in the air and my hopes for a new beginning are bursting forth, the images of growth are rampant.

The image of children growing as readers brings me great joy. I know the stories are there. I know children prosper as they are read to. I know parents will find the task enjoyable as they do it. I know the rewards are worth the effort.

My own children have grown into very different kinds of readers. Janie, my daughter, will read anything — the thicker the book, the more complicated the relationships, the better. James

Webb, my son, won't sit still very long for anything. He gets his reading done fast. *The New York Times*, *The Wall Street Journal*, the *Economist*, *Sports Illustrated*, computer manuals, the stock market report — and he's out of here. He reads on the run. Son-in-law Alan, an outdoorsman, reads *National Geographic* and all the nature magazines. He is a bathtub reader who has taught my grandchildren to do the same thing.

My grandchildren are shaping themselves into different kinds of readers. Kali is a died-in-the-wool series book reader. Baby-sitters Club, Sweet Valley Twins, Friends 4-Ever, or any other series is just right for her. Jason is a horse lover, a poetry lover, a Roald Dahl lover, an animal lover. He keeps Shel Silverstein beside his bed and escapes to his room to read animal stories while he pets his dog. Three-year-old Trisha listens to *Goodnight Moon* and *Each Peach Pear Plum* every night and will listen to almost anything you read to her for a half hour or so. They are your garden variety mix of readers.

I wonder why they are all so different. I've made it clear to every one of them that reading is important to me. As any good gardener knows, you plant the seeds, nurture them with water and sun, cultivate them to give them room to grow. But then you stand back and watch. They determine the shapes they take, the flowers they produce. Children decide which books to read and the kind of reader they become. We celebrate their differences in our bouquet of happiness.

Bernice E. Cullinan
New York University, Spring, 1993

Appendix

Books for Parents

Bialostok, Steven. *Raising Readers: Helping Your Child to Literacy.* Peguis Publishers, 1992.

Butler, Dorothy. *Babies Need Books.* Atheneum, 1980.

Cullinan, Bernice E. *Read to Me: Raising Kids Who Love to Read.* Scholastic, 1992.

Freeman, Judy. *Books Kids Will Sit Still For: The Complete Book Guide.* Bowker, 1990.

Hearne, Betsy. *Choosing Books for Children.* Delacorte, 1981.

Jett-Simpson, Mary. *Reading Resource Book: Parents and Reading.* Humanics, 1986.

Kimmel, Margaret Mary, and Elizabeth Segel. *For Reading Out Loud! A Guide to Sharing Books with Children.* Delacorte, 1988.

Lamme, Linda Leonard. *Growing Up Reading:*

Sharing with Your Child the Joys of Reading. Acropolis Books, 1985.

Larrick, Nancy. *A Parent's Guide to Children's Reading.* Dell, 1982.

Oppenheim, Joanne, Barbara Brenner, and Betty D. Boegehold. *Choosing Books for Kids: Choosing the Right Book for the Right Child at the Right Time.* Ballantine Books. A Bank Street Book, 1986.

Reed, Arthea J. S. *Comics to Classics: A Parent's Guide to Books for Teens and Preteens.* International Reading Association, 1988.

Trelease, Jim, editor. *Hey! Listen to This: Stories to Read Aloud.* Viking, 1992.

Trelease, Jim. *The New Read-Aloud Handbook.* Viking Penguin, 1992.